Into the Veil

Ayden Morse

ISBN:
979-8-9918880-2-8

I want to thank my brother, he supported and helped me finish this book

1

I took a long sip from my black coffee, the worn blue mug fitting perfectly in my hands, glancing down at them. The steam from the coffee warmed my face, and the surface of the cup kept my hands warm. When did they get so worn-looking? For just a 24-year-old, my hands looked like they had gone through shit. I gripped my cup tighter and brought it to my lips to sip the black coffee. A lock of my black hair fell into my face, so I brushed it aside and sat my cup back down, sighing. I relaxed back into the booth. The smell of grounded coffee filled the air in this little coffee shop, always putting me in a better mood. However, today, I don't think that'll be possible.

It's only been a short time since I returned to Northwood from Minneapolis. Well, I guess it's been a few months, almost a year, but the only reason I came back was due to my parents' death in a freak car accident, both gone. They told me it was quick, though that's the spiel I use for every family member I speak to about cases. Even if the death was not immediate, we still use that line. It's just better that way, and I wasn't there for my parents' crash, so I just let myself believe in what they told me. I don't think I could handle knowing if they suffered.

My emerald green eyes glanced over the newspaper across the table for the sixth time. I was a bit distracted thinking about the last year. Even with the grieving I was left to do, I wasn't handling my parent's death all too well. However, I doubt I'll ever get over it, so I buried myself in the paper, reading over the headline of my new case.

We don't get tourists often, and the two that happened to show up were killed in the local park. They just ended up in the wrong place at the wrong time. It was a murder, a strange one at that. I don't have all the details yet, but they were both killed using acid. The bodies were almost entirely unidentifiable. Okay, completely unidentifiable. The acid must have been strong since it dissolved every organic material of the two, including their clothing and items they had. Luckily, some teeth survived, though. Not lucky for the two, but the man was identified as Bruce Molina, so they called around and figured out the girl was Callie Becker. I haven't seen pictures since the newspaper only showed a picture of the trees near the area. It's not uncommon for them to do that. The image of any murder is always too graphic to show in the newspaper.

All of this happened just the other day, but with such a small town, when there is a murder, it becomes the talk of the whole community. We all stick together in such a tight-knit way, so when there is a possibility of one of us being a killer, it breaks that net freaking everyone out. And without any leads, it's making people turn on each other, so that's where I come in. Even though I am on leave due to my parents, I was called in specifically for this case. It may sound morbid, but I'm somewhat glad for the distraction, and the townsfolk need a little hope, so I'll do whatever I can to help them.

Putting the newspaper down, I lifted my mug with my left hand, drinking the rest of the coffee with a loud sigh. I pulled out my black wallet from my dark brown overcoat to place the exact change on the table. Moving to stand, my coat falling to my knees. The jacket was a hard find; I love them longer, but being six feet tall, they are usually too small for me.

Once up, I gave the small cafe a once over. I was the only one besides the dark-haired barista, who I couldn't see at the moment. He must be in the back. But since I left the money for the coffee with an added extra for him, I made my way out, passing the long counter the barista typically stands behind. At the same time, the rest of the building is filled with booths with only two tables with standard chairs. Every time I glance at all the coffee machines, I wonder how they all work, but I'm more of a coffee drinker, and I'd rather not get into that mess. They also have a little pastry spot, but everything they have is always way too sweet for me, though their muffins aren't too bad.

As I stepped out of the small cafe, the open sign clinked against the doors. Becoming blinded by the sun, I used my left hand to pull my gray Fedora down to shade my eyes so I could see my surroundings.

The small street in front of me looked worn from years of service. I turned to face the cafe. The Steamy Bean Cafe was labeled above the door in some curling font, making it hard to read, but everyone knows the place anyway. Other small stores are lined beside the cafe that make up our downtown street. It's small, but it has what we need.

Looking ahead, my brown Chevy Caprice waited in the parallel parking spot. I walked towards it using my left hand to open the door, huffing a little as I sat in my comfortable seat. I instinctively grabbed my lighter from the middle console before hesitating and returning it. "Right, no more smoking," I say aloud to the empty car. I had quit two years ago and started back up after my parent's death, but I'm trying hard to stop it. My mother always hated that habit. I got it from my father, and after seeing all the concern and fear it brought to my mother, I decided to stop it cold turkey. It's not easy, but I'm trying hard to make her proud.

I started the car and pulled forward onto Lune Street, all the stores to my right. If I had turned the car around, you'd see the apartment building and local grocery store. Still, if you kept going down the road, you'd hit a dirt patch that ended up by the freeway entrance. It's about a two-hour drive of thick trees and bumpy roads, which always made me feel like I was driving right into a horror movie.

That sums up Northwood, though we are known for the massive forest that, if anyone dares to enter, will forever be lost. There are numerous stories of cryptids. If you walked up to about anyone in this town, they would have a story to tell you. Many of them are about strange creatures that live in the woods and legends, but they're all just stories to explain why people go missing in the woods, claiming they've seen these things in person, but me? These woods are untraveled and thick. It is so easy to get turned around and lost. Wolves and bears live here, too, they may not be supernatural, but I don't believe in any of that bizarre shit. There's a reason for everything, and I'm sure my story stays true to the facts.

They tried to convince me of these things, but I had never seen anything living in this town my whole life. I would have seen something by now if any of it was true. Seeing is believing, and well, I haven't seen a damn thing. Of course, weird things happen, but it doesn't mean anything. Some townsfolk tried to convince me Bigfoot drank at the local bar. Yeah, he was a damn hairy guy, but that doesn't mean he's Bigfoot! People can be hairy, but I don't believe it without proof or hard evidence. As a detective, it's my thing.

As I get lost in my thoughts, I almost gasped when I nearly missed my turn into the parking lot of the police station, turning right into it at the last minute. The station sat alone with an entrance from the main road and one to the right of the building that leads down to the park. Still, even so, it wasn't significant. Three cars were parked here already, with one police car parked with them, so I took the spot beside the door, knowing I wouldn't be here long.

I exited the car and saw the window close to the main entrance. It went into the boss's office, the blinds shut, which was typical for him, but it made it hard to see if he was there. Placing my keys into my pockets and closing my door, I glanced around the small lot, realizing the absence of the boss's car, hoping he was using the police cruiser today.

Walking to the station's front door, I immediately saw inside because it was made of glass. Pushing against it with my sleeved arm, I enter the lobby. The room itself is a pretty decent size. To the right of me is the conference room with a glass wall to see inside, and to the right of that, beside the front doors, is the boss's office. His door shut, and the little window showed the lights were off. Damn looks like he's out.

Looking ahead, I can see the rest of the room: the restrooms to the left of me, the small desk where the receptionist works in the middle of the room, and then the back wall where the two large doors that lead to the cells, morgue, laboratory, and interrogation room.

"Hey Mill!" Kane's voice interrupts my thoughts as I turn to the left, seeing him emerge from the restroom

Kane is three years younger than me. Being 21, he works at the front desk part-time, making his way up to become a police officer. Still, for now, he handles everything needed at the front: cleaning, sorting papers, and taking calls.

He has short dark brown hair that goes past his ears and milky brown eyes with his cheeks full of freckles. I always see him dressed in professional button-up shirts and typically slacks. Today, he wore a blue shirt and black slacks, his eyes always full of light.

"How's it going today, Kane?" I asked him as I approached the front desk.

"I am doing well. How was your time off?"

"I suppose it was alright, pretty quiet, but I'm ready to get back into things."

"What did you have in mind?"

"I am certain you already know," I say as I lean against the desk. "The recent double murder. I want the documents."

"Why am I not surprised?" Kane responded as he pulled a yellow binder from beneath the desk. "This has all the info, though there isn't much here."

"That's fine. I'm headed home, so I'll go over these when I get there," I tell Kane as I take the thin binder. It felt like nothing was inside.

"What did you do all day? It will be dark out soon. You could have come in the morning?" Kane asked, tilting his head a little. He's always been too curious for his own good.

"Well, since tomorrow is technically my first day back, I spent today doing nothing. Then I got coffee," I told him with a soft smile as I glanced at the boss's office. Was the boss in at all?"

"He left an hour ago; not much is going on now, and we have hardly any evidence on the new case."

I nodded, then looked at the binder in my hands. "Before I crack this open, what do you know?" I asked with my right eyebrow raised

"Well, not much, Mill. I'm not normally out on the field, but we cannot get any samples of the murder weapon, the acid. I mean, because anything we put in it dissolves it."

"Don't we have any jars lined with ptfe?" I asked

"ptfe?" Kane questioned, looking over at me

"It's a chemical lined inside special jars so that when you put a powerful acid inside or more specifically fluoroantimonic acid, which can break down the glass, we use ptfe to more or less prevent that."

"Oh, I see, maybe Poppy has some?"

"Let's hope she does," I tell him, the room growing silent momentarily before Kane speaks up again.

"Well, I'll be back in the morning, so I'll speak with her when she comes in."

"Thanks, Kane. I appreciate that. So I'll see you bright and early then," I tell him, smiling.

"Yeah, you drive safe. I look forward to seeing you again," Kane told me, smiling wide, his dimples showing as he did

I nodded to his response, in a better mood than before. As I turned to leave, Kane waved me off and started to wipe down the desk's surface. I stepped through the front door again and headed to my car when a large white van suddenly pulled beside me: Sam's Van, a small newspaper company owned by Sam, a 27-year-old guy who is super friendly but very nosy. He has short, very blond hair and green eyes. He's wearing a white polo shirt with blue flowers and blue jeans.

"Hey Mill!" he said with that devilish smile. Sam is the first to step up whenever something happens in this town, though I can't blame him. Last week, his paper covered how the coffee shop got new flowers.

Then there's his assistant, whose name is also Sam, a nineteen-year-old girl working in the newspaper here for money and real-life experience. Though unsure how much she will learn here, she's brilliant. I've encountered her a few times, and she's almost had me talk about cases. I don't know how she does it; she mostly does photography for the paper. She has long black hair tied back into a ponytail by a pink ribbon and dark brown eyes; she wears a knee-length green dress. Her middle name is Jae, and that's how she introduces herself now to prevent confusion between them.

"You know I can't tell you anything about the hikers, right?" I tell him.

"Oh, come on, anything will do!" Sam told me.

"Why don't you pester someone else?"

"You're the only detective in town and the best. Why wouldn't I come to get information from you?"

"Well, like every other time, my answer is no. Go bother someone else.'" I tell him as I maneuver around them and walk towards my car.

"Um, Mill?" Jae asked, her voice quieter compared to Sam's voice

"Hmm?" I responded to her, turning back to face them only to jump back. She was directly behind me. Damn, she was fast.

"Are you going to find whoever did this to the hikers?"

"Oh, uh, of course. We all will. My team and I, you two don't have to worry about anything," I told Jae as I stepped back to create some room.

"Does that mean you have a lead?!" Sam asked, standing by Jae now so they were both way too close for comfort.

"Wouldn't you like to know," I tell him before getting into my car. Once inside, I noticed Sam looking frustrated. I'm sure he'll find the information he wants one way or another. I've never seen him give up. Sometimes, it gets on my nerves, but I try not to let it get to me.

Letting out a long breath to calm myself, I toss the binder into the passenger seat before starting the vehicle. I pulled out of the parking lot, back to the main road, took a right, and then just kept leaving the town entirely as trees overtook both sides of the road.

My car started to shake as I hit a spot in the road with potholes, driving for about five minutes of nothing but trees. I saw the Johnson's restaurant come into view. The most prominent restaurant in this town is a long-looking building. I could see the booths inside by the windows, but it looked pretty empty. The forest is right behind it, so the parking lot is to the right side of the building. I stop inside pretty often, but I have leftover spaghetti I need to eat.

After passing the restaurant, I drove for another mile, my car kicking dust up as I hit a pretty untouched road. I took a left onto an even dustier dirt road just wide enough for my vehicle, trees towering over me as I drove down for another mile until the trees opened up, revealing my old home.

I pull up to the front of my place. The road in front of my house is opened like a circle, and my yard starts from around the porch and spreads back behind the house. As I shut the car off, grabbing the file, I get out of the car and sigh. I don't know why, but I always get such an empty feeling whenever I come home, and I'm pretty sure it's the absence of my parents.

It's a one-story house built long ago by my great-grandfather, but it fits my small family well. The dark paint was chipping away due to age as the stairs on the front porch were slowly collapsing. My father wanted to fix all of this up, having gotten to the roof, fixing it up, and painting it a lovely warm blue with the chimney's bricks having been redone as they stick out of the right side of the house more towards the back.

Seeing the nice redone roof made me wish he could have finished it. I looked down at the file in my hands. Why am I doing this to myself? They're gone, and I couldn't do anything about it, so wishing they were here and back wouldn't change anything. I took a shaky breath and walked forward; the porch steps creaked beneath my weight, my eyes trailing up to the old rocking chair to the left of the door. It is pure white with parts of paint chipped away. I should bring this into the house sometime to keep it out of the weather, though I suppose this is where my mother liked it, so I'll probably never find a time to bring it in.

With a heavy sigh, feeling my heart ache, I try to focus back on the job at hand as I lift my left hand to open the white door, leaving it unlocked since, well, I don't have much of a need to worry about people breaking in. My nose was insulted with the smell of dust and maybe even a little bit of mold. I have a plan to fix things up; I just haven't been in the right mindset, so I'm hoping after this case, it helps with the slump I've been in so I can start taking care of things.

The house's entrance is a hallway more or less with brown wooden walls and wooden flooring, coat hooks are set to the right of me with a little stand for shoes, and a painting of some brown and white horse is above all of it with mini hooks for keys. I removed my Fedora and overcoat, kicking my brown dress shoes off as I kept the file in my left hand. I hung things up, placing my car keys on the mini hook beside a set of keys. I'm unsure where they go. A tiny little bell can be heard coming towards me.

Looking down the long hall, I see my white Persian trotting up to me. Her little bell alerts me that she is there and gives a loud, long meow.

"There you are, girl," I say to her, unable to hold my laughter as she rubs against my legs. I found Marshmallow back in the big city. She was only a kitten left abandoned on some street. I picked her up and ended up taking her home, and ever since then, it's been her and me. She has the whitest coat in the world with beautiful copper eyes.

"You hungry girl?" I asked before chuckling. "Wait, you're always hungry," I said out loud as I put the file under my right arm. I walked down the hall, turned left into the kitchen, and entered a square room with an oval wooden table and two chairs in the middle. To my right are the stove, fridge, and counter with the microwave. Cupboards are placed over them, with a mini one for the fridge and a fan over the stove. To the left, there is a window overlooking the front of the house with the sink right below it and a small counter beside it to the right with a drying rack and towel, a few dishes sitting in it, with more counter to the left of it where a blender and my coffee pot are located, the floor is white and the wall a light blue with a darker blue tile along all the counters and stove.

Marshmallow meows, still rubbing against my legs, as I placed the file on the table and reached down to pet her, feeling her purr against my left hand. "Don't worry, girl, I got you," I told her as I walked over to the right, grabbing a can of cat food from the top cupboard. She loves these things, and it showed with her little bell jingling as she got up, placing her hands on the top of the counter, trying to reach up to get it from me.

"Just a moment," I told her as I popped open the lid and dumped it into a cute little bowl. It was blue and flat. I placed it on the floor, and Marshmallow quickly ate it up. "Slow down. You don't want to puke, do you?" I asked her, though my words only went from one ear out of the other as I sighed, letting her be. She's never actually gotten sick eating her food, so I let her be as I got the spaghetti out of the fridge. It's in a glass container. I popped the lid off and placed it into the microwave to heat up. Once done, I put a fork into it and grabbed the file off the table before I left the kitchen and went back into the hallway.

I walk down to the living room, passing a couple of doors to my right. The first one leads into a bedroom, and the second into the bathroom.

I paused for only a minute when I stepped into the living room. The roof expands in this room, making it feel like a log cabin. To the right, a black pleather couch sat with a small glass coffee table in front of it and a sunflower coaster placed on it, leaving the table clear of any smudges besides the nose smudges from Marshmallow. She likes to press her nose up against the bottom of it.

The TV sits in front of the couch, a foot or so from the coffee table. It's an old bulky TV that weighs more than my fridge, I swear, with a hefty stand under it. An unused fireplace rests against the right wall; there is a ladder to the left wall, and climbing up it, you'll be on a platform-like loft. My old bed, dresser, and, well, everything is up there. When I was a kid, I had a choice of a room or a loft, and silly me; I chose a loft with a blanket hanging from the ceiling to cover it up. It's pretty empty now, besides my old bed and dresser. However, I've been staying in my parent's room, not wanting to climb a ladder whenever I want to go to bed.

Moving to the coffee table, I placed the spaghetti and file on the table and proceeded to sit, but a noise stopped me. I turned to the back door, a blast of wind hit it, alerting me that the door was cracked open. That's strange. I always lock it, but it always ends up open. I approached it, closed the door, and turned the lock. I tested it to ensure it was locked, just like before leaving the house. It's the only door that does this, and it unsettles me a lot. The backyard of my home has always made me weary as I looked out the window. The back door is made up mostly of glass, as all I can see is the mowed yard.

The spots too close to the trees are untouched since, for some reason, I didn't feel comfortable enough to get close. Maybe it's just that eerie feeling like anything is out there, the unknown. As a kid, I've seen wolves in this backyard before, so it's probably just that little bit of uncertainty. I took a long sigh, testing the door again, thankful Marshmallow was still inside. I've never had an issue with her not being inside, even if the door is cracked open, but I need to figure out why this keeps happening. But for now, I should get to work.

I gave a huff as I sat on the couch. I grabbed the remote for the TV beside me and turned it on, letting it land on some random channel. The noise droning out for me, but it was sound, and that's all I needed to keep the silence away as I made sure my phone was placed on the table from my pocket to make them empty as I grabbed the yellow file to go through, letting it sit flat against the table. I opened it up and found there wasn't much, just like Kane had told me.

I pulled out the top paper, which contained information about Callie Becker, one of the victims. It says she was nineteen years old, and the other person was Bruce Molina. He was only a year older; their families were called, leading into what little we knew. They came here to go camping, finding our woods exciting, but ended up being murdered just before they could start their journey. Being located right at the edge of the woods in the park, maybe they were going to camp out in the woods there, but regardless, they didn't make it that far.

As I kept reading, it looked like their bags were found untouched by the acid. Still, their items, wallets, money, and even their expensive gear were all untouched, which meant there was a more significant reason for this. Were they killed due to just being at the wrong place at the wrong time, or maybe whoever did this wanted to show off? I've seen a rather large group of people who kill for the most superficial reasons. I need to count them all out. We don't know what we're dealing with yet, even to have it be an accident, though I'm not entirely sure how that idea would pan out.

Sighing, I look over one last time but see nothing else. I go into the folder to grab the other piece, finding it turned upside down. I turn it around, my breath hitching in my voice. "Dear god," I mumbled under my breath, shocked it was pictures of the crime scene. No wonder they only had photos of the trees and grass; these are gruesome even for me.

It had multiple pictures set from the top view, side, front, and back of both the victims, which I am thankful for since those are the only images I will get from the crime scene. Usually, we have bodies to look over. Still, in this case, the bodies are already dissolved into nothing—they were in horrible shape even when these pictures were taken.

The two bodies are lying beside each other; the body to the right is Bruce, marked as such on the paper. At this point, Callie's face dissolves as her skull caves into itself while Bruce is getting there. Still, luckily, they were able to recover some of his teeth to identify them. It's not too lucky for them, but at least we have names for the bodies so they can have a proper burial.

Even though Bruce's face was semi-intact, their bodies weren't there, skin devolving away as veins and tendons exposed, those starting to dissolve away and turning into a mushy pile of guts and melted skin. I couldn't imagine the smell; even though these were pretty gruesome pictures, there wasn't much to go off of. The only murder weapon was acid, it seemed, and if there was any scarring or damage done before, this was all gone along with the bodies, leaving a pretty cold trail for us to follow. One small detail I couldn't overlook is the plants around the bodies dying off and browning from the crime scene; even the parts a few inches away from being touched by the acid are dying off, leaving a pretty sizable brown area of dead flora.

Looking closer, I started to realize the acid looked... Wrong? I look back into the folder to find the last piece of paper. I pulled it out, finding more close-up pictures of the scene, which helped with my suspicions. The acid was a strange black goo. I've never seen anything like this until now, but it piques my interest a lot. I need some samples of this stuff, but I must wait until Poppy can. It is much like fluoroantimonic acid. You can't just use any container, but I've never seen that stuff black like this, so maybe it's some form of new acid? After finding out how it's made, it could lead us to a suspect.

Placing all the papers down, I bite my lip, thinking over all this information. It was all I had to go off, so I'll have to work hard to find new pieces to figure out this puzzle, but I'm willing to put in all the work. I'll find the last detail and reveal the truth. I know it'll prove difficult, considering this is the town I've lived in my entire life. We do have some new townsfolk, though I can't just suspect them.

A tiny meow interrupted my thoughts, causing me to look down and see Marshmallow purring and rubbing up against my leg. "Hey girl," I spoke, giving her some pets. "You're right. It is getting late. I can focus on all of this in the morning," I say, unable to stop my smile. She always knows how to bring me into a good mood. I picked her up, laying back on the couch with her curling onto my chest. My spaghetti was forgotten and left cold on the coffee table. I put all my attention on Marshmallow, giving her lots of pets while lying on my back, and her purrs vibrated on my chest.

As I lay there, I wandered back to the case, planning my first moves to try and catch the boss in the morning to talk to him and then Poppy. Those would be my best moves to get the ball rolling. Marshmallow rubbed against my head, making me laugh a little as I looked up at her. "okay, I'll get some sleep," I told her as I yawned. I know I got a nice bed in the room, but right here at the moment, I was way too comfortable to move as I let the sounds of my cats purring and the white noise of the TV put me to sleep.

2

I felt somewhat groggy as I slowly opened my eyes. A crank in my back from the couch while Marshmallow purred, her vibrations soothing me as I gave her a soft smile, bringing a hand up to pet her as she gave a meow. She looked so comfortable and happy using me as a bed. "Good girl," I told her as I petted her, glancing over to the TV, the crackling static hurting my eyes as it was the only current light on in the house, the sun not having risen yet. Sorry, girl," I spoke in a hushed tone, shuffling a little, my tiny movement making her jump off me onto the floor, disappearing into the darkness, her little bell ringing. I reached out to the table, fumbling around before I found my phone. I knew I left it here yesterday. I always have the worst habit of leaving my phone lying around the house if it's not in my jacket. The little square device is small in my hands; the sphere is what it's called a super new kind of phone, and I'm still figuring it out. I was so used to flip phones, so having some flat phone that you tap the screen of was new. I clicked the little button to the side of it, letting it turn on, blinding me for only a second before my eyes adjusted to the light, seeing the little screen saver I had of Marshmallow, her little nose sticking into the camera never failing to bring a smile to my lips.

After adoring my cat's picture, I finally looked at the time, seeing it was 5:21 AM. The date 07/08/2000 flashed right below it, not too long before the sun will be coming out. I glanced at the back door, seeing it was still pretty dark. I always loved this time of day, before the sun rose and just before most people rose, allowing me some time of solitude to make some coffee and get to the station before it became crazy.

Stretching out, I get up from the couch before glancing down when I feel something against my leg. I see Marshmallow.

"I know, girl," I say to her softly, looking around the room. Only the

TV's light illuminates everything, so I walked over to the hallway's entrance to flick on the ceiling light, filling the room and forcing me to shut my eyes momentarily. "Damn, that's bright," I mumbled, huffing as I slowly opened my eyes. Now that I can see, I spot what I was looking for: the little colorful feather toy for Marshmallow. It sat on the floor, half under the couch, so I moved to pick it up, holding the stick part as the feather end on the string swung around.

I looked down at Marshmallow, who was on her belly, staring at the moving feather, ready to pounce. I moved the string closer to her, letting her jump at it and play around. Making me laugh as I walked to the kitchen, dragging the feather along with me. Marshmallow followed, trying to catch the feather the whole time. Once I stepped into the kitchen, I let her catch it and play with it so I could get her some food.

Reaching into the drawer, I open a new can of food and dump it into her little bowl. Marshmallow, as always, runs to it and starts to scarf it down. "You silly cat," I comment as I walk over to my coffee pot, filling it with coffee grounds and pouring some water into it using a bottle I had in the bottom drawer.

As the coffee brews, I leave the kitchen and into the hallway, deciding to go to my bedroom to get changed. Once I open the door, the cool blast of air hits me. The window across the room was left open overnight, sending a shiver up my spine. The room is a pretty nice size, the king-size bed against the back wall set in the middle of the room with white sheets and a blue blanket. A large, worn, wooded chest sat with an orange-knitted blanket before the bed.

My closet is to the left of the room. It's not very big, but it's large enough to hold all my over shirts, some of my ties, and any other random assortments of clothing with a few of my father's suits hanging in it with some boxes full of things I haven't unpacked yet. I haven't packed any of my parents' things; I'm not entirely ready to start the process. To the right of the room, I have a mini dresser for my underclothing, socks, shirts, jeans, and shorts. If I was honest, I stick primarily to my hanging clothing, so I don't know exactly what's inside. Some of my mom's glass horses sit on the dresser, dusty and old. There is a picture of some random brown horse above my bed.

A desk sat directly beside the door to the right, the surface clean for once, but it wouldn't be long once I got deep into this case. Turning back to the closet, I walked over to it and pulled off the clothing I had on, leaving my black boxers as I grabbed a light blue button-up shirt, putting it on, then black jeans before swapping out my plain black socks. The clothing I switched out of now lay on the floor to be taken care of later as I left the room.

I went into the kitchen and saw the coffee finished brewing. I grabbed my blue thermos on the counter and filled it. I took in the smell as I drank some, filling it back up before placing the lid on. I absolutely love coffee, drinking it every single day without a skip. I couldn't get through the day without it. I left the kitchen with my thermos. Moving to the front door, I slip on my shoes, setting the thermos down on the shoe rack. I slip on my overcoat, then Fedora, grabbing all my keys, when I hear a loud buzzing from the kitchen. Curious, I walk back to see my phone buzzing on the table.

"Did I leave this here?" I asked myself, confused. I had thought it was left on the coffee table?. I suppose I'm just more tired than I thought. A little weirded out, I moved forward to pick it up and found a text from Gary, which struck me as odd. He was the father to one of my closest friends growing up, though he was a little on the older side. I think he is in his seventies now. He somehow kept up with us kids.

I don't know Gary all that well. I did hang out around his place when I was a kid. When I played with his son, what was his name? Right, Jamey! He's a cool guy. I think he was one of the few who left this tiny town. Gary has lived here his whole life, much like most of us here in Northwood. I was pretty surprised he even texted me. We were never close and hadn't spoken in a relatively long time. Nothing happened between us, but I only knew him through Jamey. After we grew up, I didn't make much effort to keep in contact. Gary was a bit of a grump and scared me a little as a kid. He wasn't a bad guy, but he was never the same after Maribel, his wife, had passed. I wish I understood that when I was a kid. Maybe I could have seen where he was coming from instead of avoiding him.

I read over the text to finally see what Gary needed. I guess he wants me to come by in person to see something weird at his place before he reports it to the police. I usually would contact Scarlet, our head officer, but I figured I could just check it out. If he did it over text, it can't be that bad, right? I'll go see what has him bothered. Then, if it's worth enough, I'll call Scarlet. She's probably busy handling other things, so it's best not to waste her time.

Stuffing my phone into my jeans pocket, I head back to the front door, grabbing the thermos I had sat down and glancing down at my legs when I felt Marshmallow rub against me, giving me a tiny meow. "Sorry girl, I'll be home soon," I tell her, reaching down to provide her with a pet before leaving the house.

The early morning chill ran up my spine, giving me goosebumps. Even with my overcoat, it ran deep into my bones. I looked at the woods surrounding my home. The barely rising sun still hadn't reached the woods, making it very hard to see into them, which gave me this eerie feel in the pit of my stomach that gave me nausea. I shook my head a little to try and bring some form of focus back as I walked to my car, opened the door, and got in.

I switch my headlights on, giving me a sense of security from the darkened woods before I pull out of my driveway and down to the main street, pausing before I turn to my right, opposite from the town. Gary lived five minutes from my house, making him one of the furthest houses from town. Taking a right this time onto a dirt road much like mine but broader, it takes me three minutes to get to his old and worn home.

Gary has a two-story house. The porch in front has a design that is very similar to mine. The house was painted dark red, which has more or less chipped away from age, with the roof being a faded yellow. Honestly, even when it looked semi-new, that roof looked horrible. I will never understand why he chose yellow against red on a house. The colors clash so much. But who am I to judge?

I pull up to the front of the house to park my Chevy beside Gary's red truck. Pushing open my door and stepping out, I glanced over at his vehicle, noticing an orange liquid leaking from under the hood, and his back left tire looked completely flat. I suppose his truck needed some work, but I wasn't here for this. My eyes shifted to his house. The door itself is open with the screen door closed, keeping the bugs out, so when I walk up his porch and to the door, I knock on the wooded frame, not wanting to accidentally punch a hole through the screen.

After waiting a few minutes, Gary showed up at the door. He stood a little shorter than me, his white hair pretty much gone, though his peppered beard still somehow stayed thick, the black coloring mostly gone as his blue eyes met with my green. I could see the bags under his eyes, and damn, he looked tired; it made him look even older. Still, it could be the stressed look he had. His red flannel and his dirt-stained dark blue jeans made him look rough. The rifle he held in his hands looked familiar, the same one he kept by the door in case of bears or other wildlife, so it unnerved me he would answer the door holding it.

His expression went from worry to surprise when he registered it was me. "Oh! Mill, I didn't think you would show up so early!" he told me, his voice raspy as if he hadn't spoken in a while.

"Of course, I came. It sounded important, but... Gary, you look so tired," I commented. I knew he was an older guy, but he never looked this tired, as if he was neglecting himself.

"Well, I'm hoping you can give me a little relief with something that's been happening."

"Of course, Gary, I'm happy to lend a hand in any way I can. I want you to feel safe," I told him as he led me inside the house. I wasn't sure what it was, but it almost seemed the surrounding area had brightened up as if the presence of another fixed the gloom that had washed over this house.

Inside Gary's home, the warmth made me feel comfortable. It was a lot warmer than my home as I looked around the kitchen I now stood in, a wall directly to my left with a hallway right in front of me with the right side having all the kitchen items, fridge, stove, and counters, a small rounded table in the middle of it with four chairs.

"So I know I called you in to look at something, but Mill, it feels like forever since I've seen you in person. How are you?" Gary asked, glancing my way, catching me off guard. I wasn't expecting him to go into questions.

"Oh, I've been well. Returning to Northwood has been weird, but I'm adjusting alright."

"I suppose it can't be easy. . ." Gary trailed off. "Your father and I got along rather well. I couldn't believe the news."

"It's okay, Gary. How's your family?" I asked, wanting to change the subject. I wasn't entirely ready to have that conversation.

"Oh yeah, you remember Jamey? He's finally a history teacher, and my daughter is in her last year of medical school in Idaho. I'm so proud of all of them," he told me, a smile washing over his lips. I remember the last time I spoke to Gary before I had left Northwood. He wasn't on the best terms with his kids, so seeing him smile about his kids and talk about his family made me happy.

"To be honest, Mill," Gary started, "I know I wasn't the most pleasant back in the day and for such a long time, but I realized how much that affected my relationship with my family. I hardly spoke to them, and they both have kids of their own now. I couldn't stand not knowing my grandkids, so I decided to try harder and be there for them like I wasn't before, and all I can say is I'm thankful they let me be a part of their lives. I love them all."

"That's good to hear. I'm happy for you," I told him, smiling, being truthful in what I said. Gary deserved to be in contact with his kids and grandkids.

There was a pause as I noticed Gary fidgeting with the red crochet tablecloth. "G. ." I started, but he cut me off before I could say anything. The whole mood of the room changed as Gary seemed ready to tell me what had been bothering him.

"It all started a few days ago. At first, I didn't pay it much mind. You see dead critters here and there, a few birds and mice; we live far out. I see many rodents and animals dying just because of diseases or predators, but it all changed the other day. I thought something was off, but I just ignored the signs. Mill... I'm starting to get worried."

"What's going on around here?" I asked, furrowing my brows, concerned about his story. If he's seeing an increase in dead animals, our killer might be out here putting Gary in grave danger.

"I don't think I can explain it to you. But I can show you," he told me as I saw him standing up from his seat. His legs shaking as he moved made me wonder if it was due to his age or out of fear.

"Are you okay?" I asked him, unable to help but worry about his health as I stood up.

"Yeah, it's just my old bones. Nothing to worry about. Come, what I need to show you is outside."

I nodded as I followed him to the front door, the both of us stepping outside. I instantly noticed a black Chevy parked beside Gary's truck.

I walk down the steps closer to the Chevy to take a peek inside, but I only see bottles of oil for cars and a red dream catcher in the front rearview mirror.

"MILL," a voice called out, quickly grabbing my attention. I whipped around towards the left of the house, where I could see Coby headed my way. His bald head reflected light whenever the sun hit it, and from this distance, I couldn't see his blue eyes, but I could see the stains on his blue mechanic outfit.

No wonder I didn't recognize the truck. Coby must have gotten a new one to fix up and use before he sells it, just like every other car he has ever owned.

Coby is a good friend of mine; he's in his forties and the best mechanic in town, but that may be because he's our only mechanic. Regardless, he does know what he's doing.

"What are you up to?" I asked, a little suspicious since I saw him walking from the backyard. Why didn't he come to the front door of the house? I wandered as I walked to meet him halfway.

"Oh, I came by to fix up Gary's truck. You probably saw the state it's in. I was just looking around for the extra tires he said he had, but I can't find them," he told me as he crossed his arms. "Sorry if I spooked ya."

"Oh, right. I'm sorry, Coby," Gary started. I forgot I had called you. Don't you remember the truck tires are in the shed?" he asked, gesturing to the other side of the house.

"Oh, right, thank you. I'm going to get on that. Don't mind me. You two go do whatever you're doing. I'll be in the front," Coby told us as he walked past and headed to the shed.

"Well, thanks, Coby. I appreciate the help. Once you're done, please come see me."

"Yes, sir!" Coby exclaimed, not bothering to turn around and look at us as I looked back at Gary

"Shall we go?" I asked Gary, who gave me a slow nod and led me toward the backyard.

"It's right up here," Gary told me as I followed beside him, my eyes watching the untamed grass go by as it brushed against my ankles. I should come up sometime and mow his lawn for him. Just because he's older doesn't mean he should have such an untamed yard. I bet Gary would like a freshly cut yard.

"I enjoy walking around. It's where I get most of my exercise in the morning. Still, the other day, I almost fell into... Well, you'll see," he told me, almost sounding as if he was struggling to find the words, so I simply nodded and followed, making it closer to the edge of the woods when a smell suddenly insulted my senses; it was like a pile-up of mice died in a wall and were left to rot for months. The overbearing smell of rot made me gag, so I covered my mouth and nose to keep whatever was inside my stomach from coming up.

"Here it is," Gary broke the silence as he stopped. I don't know how he got this close without covering at least his nose as I moved to stand right beside him, seeing a puddle of black goo on the grass. It was slowly dying as if the goo was sapping the life from the plants. Looking into the puddle, I could see a rabbit. Almost entirely dissolved with its guts spilled out of its belly, I could see one of its eyes still formed as it was half melted into the acid. The white fur, the only thing showing it was a rabbit, while squirrels, chipmunks, and even birds meet the same fate in the giant puddle.

Wanting to examine it closer, I knelt at a reasonable distance, avoiding touching the goo, well, acid by my guess, with how it dissolves these animals. The smell of their rotting flesh punched me in the face. God, this was awful. Covering my mouth didn't help as my stomach threatened to spit up its contents, so I swallowed hard and tried to stay professional. Leaning over to grab a stick close by, I used it to lift what was left of the body, lifting it to look inside. The rabbit fell apart from the pressure, the acid breaking down too much of its body to keep any form, clumps of fur dissolving into the goo from what fell apart.

"What do you think, Mill?" I heard Gary from behind me as I turned to look behind me. He stood a little far from the puddle, which I don't blame him one bit. This stuff smelled awful.

"I think it smells like a donkey's ass, but this raises some red flags. It's just like what happened at the park with those two campers," I tell him as I stand up with a groan.

"But I don't understand, Mill. If this is connected, why would they kill such Innocent creatures right after killing two people?"

"Well, I don't exactly have an answer to that, but they may have been targeting animals, and those two campers just ended up In the wrong spot at the wrong time. I could be wrong. But I won't know until I get more evidence," I tell him as I walk closer to where he stood and away from the animals, where the air feels cleaner.

"I do suggest staying indoors for the time being, Gary. I know you like your morning walks, but stay indoors and keep your doors locked. However, I suggest maybe going to the inn, at least until this is all sorted out," I told him, concerned for his safety. I can't let Gary get injured, at least if I can prevent it. I feel safer if he stayed in the town's motel for a few days while I figure this out.

"It's okay. I don't want to leave my home. I'll stay, but keep the doors locked and be careful."

I frowned, not liking his answer, but I had no authority to tell him what to do. If he wanted to stay home, I couldn't force him otherwise as I opened my mouth to speak when a sound caught my attention, making me close my mouth to listen. However, it fell silent, and I turned my head towards the forest not far from us. Did I hear something? It could have just been my imagination, I suppose? It just sounded so real, like a song that was playing. It was quiet yet easily chosen from the wind and sounds of critters chirping, standing out like a white tiger.

"What is it?" Gary asked since I had gone silent, my eyes fixated on the woods

"I thought I heard something," I told him, trying to focus when I heard it again. "There it is," I whispered so I could listen to the song.

It was still hard to make out, but it was definitely there. I didn't imagine anything. The music sounded as if it came from a bagpipe. The song was sorrowful and beautiful, but something was off. It was hard to place, but the instrument sounded like it had been dunked in a lake with a wetness. Still, though, it was hauntingly beautiful. It was quiet as it echoed deep in the woods until it was gone. I waited a few minutes, but I couldn't hear it at all anymore.

"Who in their right minds would be playing music out in the woods!?" Gary asked, his forehead covered in wrinkles as he furrowed his brows.

I bit my lip, concerned, as I took a few steps closer to the woods to try and see if the music would show back up, but it was to no avail. It was gone. Gary heard it, too, so I wasn't imagining it, but it was strange. Who would do this? Was it the killer? I can't just run into the woods mindlessly, not with how thick they were. I would need backup.

"Come on, Gary, you should get back into the house. I'm going to contact the others," I told him, wanting to get Gary indoors to be sheltered. I pulled my phone out from my overcoat, groaning as I saw I had no bars. I will have to get closer to town to make any calls.

"Are you going to send anyone over to keep an eye on my house?" Gary asked as I led him towards his back door to get him inside faster.

"Don't worry, I'll make sure someone patrols around. For now, stay inside, okay?" I told him as we stopped by the back door, Gary moving to open it.

"Okay, yeah, I'll do that, thank you Mill." He told me, a soft smile crossing his lips. I returned it, wanting to bring ease to him as I watched him step inside his home, disappearing from my view as I waited a moment, hoping he would listen to me and stay indoors.

With a heavy sigh, I glance back at the woods, almost expecting the music to start back up. After a few minutes of nothing, I turn and head back around the house. The absence of Coby's car was noticeable, but Gary's car did have a new tire. He worked fast. I thought I would get to talk with him. I suppose another day. He always seems busy with some car or truck.

Moving to get into my car, I turned it on; the images of those animals were fresh in my mind as I pulled out. I turned the car around to head back onto the main road.

I drove down the main road, struggling to focus. I couldn't make connections between the campers and Gary's backyard unless there weren't supposed to be any, and whoever was doing it was trying to make us chase our tails.

I really hope someone over at the station has something new for me because I am not entirely sure what to make of the clues I have, if I can even call them clues.

Feeling a headache form in my temples, I finally reach the station. I pulled up like always so I could park close to the door. Four police cars were parked in the lot, which meant all the officers, including the Boss, were most likely here. It will be nice to see their opinions on what I found today. Turning my vehicle off, I stepped out, ensuring my keys were in my pockets before entering the building. The first thing I noticed was the silence. Kane wasn't there, so there was no one to greet me, giving off an eerie feeling.

I walked over to where the Boss's office was located. The tiny window inside the door was covered with a cloth, and trying the knob, it was locked, which I found odd I don't recall him typically locking the door, so I gave it a knock.

"Mill?" a sudden voice behind me, startling me as I whipped around to see whose voice it was, only to see the Boss walking my way. It seemed he had come through the door at the end of the room. What was he doing there? Looking him over, his dark brown hair looked greasy, like he hadn't showered in a few days. His hazel eyes had this dim look as if glazed over. The black suit he was wearing looked new.

"What's going on?" I asked

"I tried calling you multiple times, but you never answered your phone?" He said, "I got everyone in the back. We're having a meeting."

"Oh, I was up at Gary's. I actually have some information I want to..." he cut me off. "Well, you can tell me when we are in the back room with everyone."

I gave him a nod, not a fan of how he spoke to me as if I was a child. Examining him a little closer, he looked as if he was sweating, as if he had run a few miles to get here. The room we stood in was air-conditioned and, honestly, a little chilly.

"Well, let's get to the meeting, shall we?" I spoke up to prevent any long silence from forming.

"Good idea," Boss replied as we headed to the back door. His first name is Robert, but we all call him Boss.

With my right arm, I pushed the door open as we walked into a hall. The first thing I spot is the door at the end of the long corridor that leads to steep stairs into the morgue. Directly to my right is a heavy door with a keypad, a large window beside it looking into Poppy's room, where she does all her sciency things and deals with bodies before they go into a morgue. Three cells line up to the left of the hall. At the same time, the fourth door leads into an office that is also used as an interrogation room. However, I can't remember ever having to interrogate someone in there.

The two of us head to the last room on the left, the door already open, letting Boss walk past me to the front of the whiteboard at the end of the room. I can see Kane seated at the large, rounded table in the middle of the room in a chair closest to the door. He wore a nice salmon-colored button-up shirt and dark blue jeans, his hair sticking up a little. When he saw me, he gave a giant smile and pointed to the seat to his right as he pulled it out a little, so I moved to sit beside him.

To the left of me, on the other side of Kane, is Scarlet. She's second in command and excellent at her job, the two of us going pretty far back. She's currently in her blue police outfit. Her long amber hair is tied back into a ponytail as she glances at me, giving a soft smile, her hazel eyes like sunflowers.

"It's good to see you," She told me.

"Same to you, Scarlet," I told her, returning the smile as I leaned on the table.

This was when Ryker spoke up. He sat somewhat across from me at the table. Working as Scarlet's partner, the two work rather well together. I see he's also in a police outfit, his green eyes meeting mine, his light brown hair shaved close to the skull. "It's a good thing you showed up. Something came up that you need to hear," he said.

"What is the news?" I asked Ryker, but instead of him, I heard Benny talk as I turned around in my chair to see him leaning against the wall almost directly behind me. He's the quiet type, standing just a little taller than me at 6" 2, his black overcoat reaching past the hips of his dark blue jeans and wrinkled teal shirt.

"It's something to do with Margy," Benny explained, meeting my eyes. His blue eyes glazed over. He's a police officer, too, but he works as an interrogator. Though it doesn't come up often, he just helps Scarlet and Ryker.

"Why don't we let the boss talk?" Poppy mentioned, the last person in the room. She stood in front of the whiteboard beside Boss, our morgue attendant and the one who looked over the evidence. She's relatively intelligent, having an insane degree in the science field. Still, for some reason, she puts all of that effort here. With a brain like hers, she could work in one of the best places if she wanted, but I'm glad she works here. She is pleasant to work with and very helpful on cases. Her iconic red hair was messy as she wore a white hoodie and orange skirt that fell to her ankles. Her gray eyes were full of light.

"Thank you, Poppy," the Boss said as he looked over the police team. "I received a call from Margy just before this meeting. I suppose she's been finding her cats dead and told me that she keeps finding the dead cats in a sort of black goo. I suspect it's the same that the two campers were found in, but we will need you Mill to inspect it. Take some jars with you to collect it for Poppy," he told me.

"Understood, but I should tell you I was at Gary's. He has a lot of forest critters dead in the same matter, but we also heard a sort of bagpipe in the woods just before I left."

"Music?" Poppy asked, raising an eyebrow. "Someone was just out playing music in the middle of the woods? Who would do that?"

"Maybe someone who likes to kill small creatures?" I bring up, "The campers could have very well been a mistake, a trap set for the animals, and they happen to fall in it?"

...The room was silent. This new information only complicates things

"Regardless," Boss spoke, "Mill, I want you to go to Margy's and check out the property for any clues. We will need anything you can bring up. We don't know what this person is up to, but we can't mark anything off until we have hard evidence."

Benny lifted a hand after Boss was done talking. "I could always go up and patrol Gary's house. Hang out for a few hours off and on to make sure things are okay?" he suggested

"I think that's a good idea," Scarlet said. "Ryker and I can handle patrolling the town easily enough. It's not a whole lot of ground anyways."

The Boss nodded as he tapped his chin. "Okay, then, Scarlet, you handle the patrolling during the day, and Ryker, you go get some sleep. I'll have you on night duty. Benny will handle Gary's property and help in town if needed. I will stay here to handle incoming calls and jump into action if anything goes wrong, Mill. You go to Margy's to gather any information and, oh, take Kane with you."

I could see Kane grow excited beside me, a smile growing. "Really, sir?!" He asked Boss as he placed his hands on the table. I felt slightly unsure of this since I was used to working alone. I glanced at the Boss. Our eyes met for only a second, but it was hard to read them. They were so glazed over. Something felt off about them, but I couldn't place it.

"I suppose that is fine as long as he doesn't get in the way," I tell him, nodding.

"You won't have to worry about anything!" Kane told me, smiling

"I will do everything I can to ensure we solve this case!"

Oh, I couldn't turn him down now. Damn, I've never seen him smile so big before, unable to stop the slight smile on my lips. "I don't doubt it a bit," I tell him.

"Alright, everyone understands their assignment? Let's get going. We have a lot of work and only so much sun!" Boss announced, his voice echoing off the walls.

I used the table to pull myself up as I saw Kane quickly stand. Ryker left relatively quickly, probably heading straight home to get some sleep while the rest slowly left. However, Poppy paused, stepping over to me.

"Hey, Mill, real quick, here are the bags you need to use to collect samples," she said, handing me a small blue bag.

"Oh! Thank you, these will definitely come in handy," I say, taking them.

"Thanks. Good luck out there," She said before leaving the room. I turned my gaze at Kane, who looked rather eager to get going.

"It's not going to be all fun, you know that, right? It'll probably be boring if anything," I told him, ensuring he was not getting his hopes up only to end up disappointed.

"Don't worry, I know this just gives me a chance to learn under someone super awesome!" he exclaimed, which made me a little embarrassed. I'm not used to being called extraordinary or anything of the sort.

"I'm not that cool. I just do my job; if you stick to it, you'll be good at it, too. Now come on," I told him, leading us out before he could ask or say anything, needing to focus on the task at hand.

"Well, I think you're pretty neat," Kane said from behind me as he followed me.

"Oh, thank you," I said, embarrassed as I rubbed the back of my neck. Passing Poppy's room, I saw she was already back in her little room. Papers were all over the middle table meant for bodies. Still, she was using it for storage, as the counters against the walls were full of items. Getting to the lobby, I caught sight of the Boss's office. It looked like Benny was speaking to him, but all I could see was Benny's back.

I was not in the mood to bother them, so I left with Kane to go to my car. Getting inside, I start it up before pulling out of the parking lot and taking a left towards the town.

3

We drove through downtown and then a mile further. To my right was Coby's car shop. I could see three cars parked up front and the garage door open with that same Chevy he had before. He must be working on it.

Right next to the shop is the small 15-room motel, the Cozy Cabin, owned by Jessy. He inherited the motel after his parents passed away a few years ago, much like what happened to mine. He's been pretty supportive since I lost mine. He's such a nice guy.

As we grew closer, I saw two very familiar cars... 'It couldn't be?' I thought, but I had to check.

"Sorry, I gotta stop here for a minute," I tell Kane, pulling into the driveway between the purple and black Toyota truck and red Nissan. Oh yeah, I know who owns these cars. Once parked, I got out of the vehicle. Kane followed suit as he gave me a questioning look.

"Who's cars are those?" Kane asked before I could push open the door

"Luke and James," I tell him, pushing the door open before he can ask any more questions.

Inside wasn't big at all; the rooms were outside of the building, so within the office was a cluttered desk at the back with a wall of keys behind it and paintings of forests lining the dark red walls. There is a bathroom to the right of the desk. Jessy stood behind the desk. His golden hair fell to his shoulders, he wore a light brown uniform shirt with the motel's name written in black on the left corner with black slacks. He looked professional as ever, his blue eyes showing nothing but kindness.

To the left of him, at the desk, is James. He and I were best friends growing up, though I don't see him all too often anymore. He left Northwood around the same time I did, but he returns once a year or so to see his mother, Margy.

He stands taller than Jessy and me. His light brown hair curls as it sits just over his ears, his green eyes meeting mine as a smile forms from ear to ear. His outfit consists of blue jeans and a black short-sleeved shirt with an outline of a white wolf.

Luke stood to the right of James, an arm on the counter as he turned to face me, the shortest of the group. His once sandy blond hair looked to have been dyed black, matching his gray eyes. He still lived here in Northwood on his father's property, which had been passed down for centuries. His father had been this town's mayor before he passed away. Luke took over the job just like his father.

Luke, James, and I have been best friends since we were kids. The three of us were inseparable, and sometimes, I wish we could go back to those simpler times. Though I am just thankful, I can still see my best friends.

"Look who the cat dragged in!" Luke exclaimed, smacking the counter. "I'm honestly shocked to see you."

I smiled softly. "What can I say? Your crappy cars gave you away," I joked

"You're one to talk," James chimed in. "you've had that Chevy forever. At least we've upgraded."

"What can I say? It runs well," I tell them.

Jessy spoke up, "While you guys chat, I'm going to get your room ready, James."

"Oh, you don't have to worry. I would hate to make you work," James responded.

"It's part of the job. Besides, I just got to ensure it's not dusty."

"Well, okay, thank you."

"What are you two doing here?" I asked after Jessy left the lobby.

"I'm staying here for a few days," James told me. "My mom isn't feeling all too well, so I'm in town to help out, though with her millions of cats, I have to stay here to avoid a major allergy reaction."

"I saw his car and stopped by," Luke said with a short laugh.

"Well, good timing, I suppose," I say, crossing my arms. "Kane here and I are headed to Margy's. She made a call with a possible clue to our case," I tell them.

"Oh! The campers?" Luke asked, "What could she possibly have all the way out there?"

"She's okay, right?" James asked, his brows furrowed.

"She's fine, don't worry,"

"Maybe I should take her to the motel for a few nights," James spoke as he rubbed his temples.

"I doubt she'll leave those cats," I tell him.

"I know... I just worry; her mind hasn't been the same since the accident."

Luke placed a hand on James's shoulder. "hey, it's okay if Mill's on the case. He'll figure it out."

"Yeah. . ." James said, though he still seemed worried. I can't blame him, though. After his dad passed away, his mom got pretty sick and has only gotten worse.

"You guys get back to what you're doing. Kane and I are going to get back to our job. I just had to see you two. It feels like forever since the three of us got together," I say

"We should go out for coffee sometime soon before James heads back to the city," Luke suggested

"I agree to that one," James said, his smile back, though faltering.

I gave a soft smile myself. "Yeah, I would like that a lot. Let's get together hopefully after I crack this case," I say with a little bit of a cocky attitude. I don't know what it was, but those two always made me feel as if I could be cocky or just more confident than I usually am.

"Looking forward to it pal!" Luke said as I started for the door,

"I'll see you guys," I said before Kane and I stepped outside.

"They seem nice," Kane said as we headed to the car.

A door to one of the far-off rooms looked propped open. I bet it gets boring running a motel in such a small town.

"They are pretty cool," I told him as we entered the car. Starting it up, I pull out onto the road.

Driving down the road, I see the small squared grocery store to the right. It used to be pretty small, but over time, it was rebuilt to be larger as more people moved here. A large sign, "The Forest Shop," is placed above the doors; the place wasn't even locally owned. The gal who owns it lives in the big city, so the store manager, Debby, handles everything.

To the left of the road is the two-year-old apartment building, which was built by a small company. They are trying to establish some ground here before the town gets popular. I've heard a few people out of town are already moving in.

Turning on the road by the apartment building, I followed the path for about five minutes until the schools came into view.

The middle and elementary school is one building on the left side of the road, while the high school is on the right, opposite each other. The middle and elementary schools are named Northwood Middle, while the high school is named Northwood High.

I always thought the names were silly, but in a small town, I guess it doesn't matter as I drove past the two.

"Hey, Mill," Kane started, "I don't know Margy all that well. What sort of illness does she have?" He asked

"Oh, well, there was an accident just before I left Northwood; she had taken a pretty harsh fall down a set of stairs and damaged bits of her brain," I explained.

"Oh. . .that's awful," Kane said

"Yeah. . she always told us stories about fairies and things living in the woods by her home. I used to love listening to them, but after her accident, she talks about these stories as if they're real, like... Reality is all messed up for her."

"Oh. ." I could tell he was a little lost for words

"Hey, sorry I probably said too much. She's a wonderful lady. She's just had a pretty rough time."

"No, it's fine. I'm glad you told me. Knowing the situation lets me know what to say and do," Kane said.

"There ya go," I told him, smiling as we drove onto a rough dirt path at the end of the road. The trees had been cut to make a tunnel deep into the woods, the path thin as my car complained against the potholes and roots that kept growing until we arrived at a small open spot. Margy's house is a small two-story home painted in a lovely white that looks fresh, no doubt because of James, and the roof is an excellent black. She has a half porch on her house that leads up to her door, which covers only the right side of the front, with two white rocking chairs.

She has a decent-sized backyard and a tiny front yard from which I had to park a fair distance due to all the items scattered all over the property. I forgot how much of a hoarder she was as I saw a black cat run across the tall grass that hadn't been mowed in a long while. I'm sure James has tried, but Margie believes things besides her cats live in the grass, so she won't let anyone touch it.

"Wow, it looks abandoned," Kane said

"It's not; Margy just likes to live in a more nature-filled environment," I told him as I exited the car.

Looking down at the ground, I see a lot of old mini houses all in different colors and sizes. The fairy homes Margy placed out definitely have seen better days as other items scattered around: garbage, stones, glass, and just an assortment of things. I saw part of a sink and an old molded stuffed duck near my car. Glancing over to Kane, who was looking back and waiting on my first move, I started to walk towards the house, cats running out of the grass as we spooked them passing by.

"Man, she has a lot of cats," Kane pointed out.

"Yeah. .. It started out as only a few, but none of them were fixed," I explained as we got closer to the house, but Kane gripped my shirt, preventing me from moving forward one foot on the porch just before I could step onto it.

"Mill, look," I turned to look at him, who had let go of my shirt and kneeled. I realized a tiny patch in the grass wasn't growing, so I leaned down and saw what looked like a pile of salt, following the path with my eyes. It led to the right and left as far as I could see, almost as if circling the house.

"I don't remember this?" I tell Kane

"It looks like a salt circle. Aren't these supposed to keep like ghosts or demons in?" he asked.

"They supposed to keep them out, at least according to most of the shows I've watched," I explained, moving to stand.

"I can't imagine the amount of salt it would take to do this," Kane told me.

"She believes in fairies, so maybe Margy is starting to see other things too?" I spoke, though I wasn't entirely sure myself.

"Do you think salt circles really work?" Kane asked, standing up

"Nah, it's just some folk's tale from long ago," I tell him, making my way to the porch.

"Hmm," Kane murmured. I paused by the door, seeing a few crosses and a horseshoe up on the wall to the left, glancing at Kane for a moment before I used my left hand to knock on the door.

After several long minutes, Margy finally answered the door. As soon as it was open, I could smell the cats instantly forcing me to take in a gasp of air, my lungs burning; three of the felines ran past me out of the house while a bunch could be seen inside. Looking at Margy, she has a little orange cat in her thin, worn arms. She looked so old for someone in their sixties. It was unbelievable. Her hair was already as white as snow, tired green eyes looked between Kane and me. Her light pink dress passed her knees with scratches throughout it. She has blue-worn slippers.

"Oh, hello, I wasn't expecting any company," she told us with a warm smile that didn't match her eyes.

"Margy, you called the station about finding your cats dead?" I half asked, hoping to jog her memory.

She gave me a blank stare as if I had grown a second head until I saw something click in her eyes. "OH! My dear, I'm sorry, yes! My poor darlings, I was out doing my rounds to make sure everyone out in the grass was doing fine when I found some of my poor kitties had been killed. Oh, Mill, it's awful. Please, you need to help ensure no more of them suffer!"

"Don't worry, Margy, we are here to help. Just tell us where you found them," I told her.

"They are in the back, right in the middle of the grass. It destroyed one of my fairy homes and killed five of my cats," she explained, looking up at me with tearful eyes. "Please make sure they are not suffering. I couldn't stand seeing them like that," Margy sobbed.

"Hey, please don't cry. You go back inside. We are going to take a look," I tell her.

"Thank you so much," Margy cried as I started to move back,

signaling Kane to follow.

"Come on, let's figure this out so we can put her at ease," I tell him

"I sure hope we can. I feel pretty bad for her."

I sighed and nodded, walking around her house, stepping over the mini-houses and dodging cats.

"Hey, how come these are different?" Kane asked as I turned to face him. He was pointing to some little square blocks with tiny doors.

"Oh, those are spirit homes. She told me little spirits would use them to nap until moving on again. Most are by the creek, but I suppose she placed a few over here, too."

"Oh. . . It's kinda cute, little homes for creatures."

"I suppose they are cute, but they sit empty, waiting for something that will never come."

"You don't believe in this stuff, huh?"

I shake my head. "no, I need evidence of their existence, and since there isn't, I don't believe."

"I see what you mean, but I like to imagine they are real."

"It's a cute concept, but it's impossible for any mythical beings to exist."

"Oh. . ." Kane said, almost sounding disappointed, but before I could console him, a god-awful smell hit me, much like at Gary's. The smell of rotting flesh insulted my senses.

"Oh god, what is that smell!?" Kane asked, covering his nose

"It's the cats," I tell him plainly as I walk forward, following the smell until a patch of dead grass comes into view. The untouched tall grass shields the horrors within the dying parts; the smell only intensifies, so I cover my mouth and nose with my sleeve.

We stood a few feet from the house, the edge of the woods, not far from the patch, almost making me hesitate, a sinking feeling hitting my stomach suddenly. Still, it was probably just the smell causing me to feel ill.

I turn to Kane, who stood not far behind me, waiting on my command. "You can stay here if you want. I won't make you see the cats." I told him he was still fresh on this job and didn't want to traumatize him.

He only gave me a nod, his sleeve pressed tightly against his mouth and nose, trying to ward off the smell.

Satisfied, I turned back to the grass and stepped forward.

Careful of where my foot landed, I quickly found the source of the smell. A large puddle of black acid sits in the middle of the dead grass. Breathing into my sleeve, trying to prevent myself from vomiting, I knelt to take a better look.

Five cats in total lay in the acid. A white one looked dissolved entirely, leaving only bits of fur and half of its head. While a gray one lay on its side still semi-together, its stomach looked as if it exploded, intestines laying out from the stomach, dissolving rapidly faster than the rest.

A light brown and white cat lay close to each other as if they had tried to climb over each other, intertwined as their bodies melded together as they dissolved. The white one's skull was gone, while the light brown's stomach flayed open, its contents wrapped around the other cat.

And lastly, a turtle shell-colored cat laid smack in the middle of the puddle on its belly, clumps of its fur gone as if it had squirmed and moved about in the acid until succumbing to its horrific death.

"Who could be doing this?" Kane choked out as he came a little closer, keeping some distance.

"That is why we are here," I responded, pulling out the bag Poppy had given me. I opened it up and went through it until I found the vile and the tweezers. No way am I putting my hands anywhere near that shit. Carefully, I used the tweezers to hold the vile and then scooped some of the acid, using a rag to wipe it off. I Dropped it into the puddle, not wanting to risk touching it as I placed the glass lid on the vile, securing it before putting it back into the bag and back into my overcoat as I stood up and backed up, taking in a few breaths once I was away from the smell.

Kane moved beside me, taking in deep breaths. "I don't understand how someone could hurt such innocent things."

"There are some sick people out there," I told him.

"Well. . .We'll put a stop to them."

"That's the attitude," I spoke, pausing momentarily before speaking again. "We should get this sample to Poppy."

"Yeah! I wanna watch her do all that science stuff."

"She does do some cool stuff," I spoke, though I doubted she would let anyone watch. She wasn't a big people person, and I knew she preferred working alone.

"You two thirsty?" Margy's voice suddenly broke the silence, startling me as I quickly turned to see her holding two cups of what I presumed to be water. For a lady who struggled with getting around, she was sure light on her feet.

"You should be inside where it's safe," I tell her

"Don't worry, honey; the fairies help guide me safely."

"Margy. . ." I spoke softly, biting my lip to prevent myself from saying the wrong thing. "Okay, well, the fairies should know it's too dangerous out here," I tell her, walking over. "Thank you for the drinks, but you should really be getting back into the house," I added as I took the drinks she handed me, moving them to Kane as I gently took Margy's right arm in my left to guide her back to the house preventing her from seeing even a glimpse of what happened to a few of her cats.

"Deary, I can get to the house without your help, even without the fairies. I'm not that gone yet," she told me.

"I know. . .I just care about you."

"I appreciate that, but really, I'm fine."

"I know you are," I tell her as the three of us get to the porch, letting her arm go. Margy turned to face me.

"I'm not the one you should be worried about," she spoke

"Who should I be worried about then?" I questioned as she placed her hands on both my shoulders, forcing me to bend down to face her. When did she get so strong?

"You are Mill. They tell me the vial is breaking, and you will be in danger!"

I looked at her, my brows furrowed with worry, "What do you mean, Margy?"

"NO! Mill, you must understand!" She raised her voice as I felt her nails dig into my skin painfully. "Please, Mill, you have to believe me. I know you all think I'm crazy, but please, you're in deep trouble!"

"Margy, please, you're hurting me," I groaned as she loosened her grip. "I'm sorry, I just need you to be careful, okay? Something will happen, and I need you to be ready."

"What are you trying to warn me of?" I asked her, disoriented. She has never yelled at me like this before.

"the border between our worlds is tearing apart by something evil, and if you keep going by this path, this evil is going to kill you," she spoke with a clarity I haven't seen in ages, her voice filled with haste, freaking me out more than it should have.

This freakout was new. Her hallucinations seem to be getting worse. I will have to let James know it might be time for him to take her someplace to get the care she needs. Taking a deep breath, I looked into her green eyes before fully standing up and making her let go.

"I'll be careful, promise."

She nodded, seeming to have calmed down a little now

"You stay indoors and safe, okay? And I promise I'll be careful," I reassured her.

She smiled at me, seeming satisfied with that answer. "Come back for tea again when you can. I'd love to see you again," she spoke as if nothing had happened, back to her old self.

"Yeah, I'll do that," I tell her, trying to usher her back into the house.

"Bring your friend too," She spoke, referring to Kane

"I'd love to," Kane said, staying behind me and out of the way as I stood in front of Margy, keeping her from wandering away from the house.

"You be careful, Margy. We better head off," I tell her, stepping off the porch.

"Alright, I'll see you boys again soon." She waved us off, and I watched her walk into the house, hesitating a moment before I turned to head to the car.

It was quiet between us for a few minutes as we stumbled through the yard, trying to avoid the tiny houses and debris scattered about until we got to the front where my Chevy is. A black cat sitting on the hood, so I got into the car and honked my horn, three cats scattering from the vehicle.

"You got those cats spooked," Kane commented, sitting in the passenger seat.

"Better spooked than dead," I replied, looking back at the house, worried about Margy. I know for a fact I don't have service right now, but once I do, I'm calling someone. Margy needs to either leave or, at the very least, have someone keep an eye on her.

"So. . ." Kane began, looking my way as I glanced at him. "What do you think she meant?"

"About what?" I asked as I pulled the car out, still focused on Margy's health.

"She said something about a veil?" he said

"Oh, right. It's nothing to worry about. She's always talking about some mythology or supernatural thing, though this time was a little concerning. She never looked so. ."

"Scared?" Kane finished

"yeah, I think it's time James moves back or takes her someplace safe."

The car fell silent again as I pulled onto the road to head back into town.

"Are you hungry?" Kane suddenly asked

"Hungry?" I asked, realizing I hadn't eaten anything that day. The thermos I made with coffee was a distant memory as I tried to remember where it was left. "I haven't had anything," I tell him.

"Why don't we stop at Johnson's? They got a sale going on right now."

"Hmm, I don't know. We should head to the station," I tell him

"But neither of us have eaten. What if something happens and we can't focus because we are too busy worrying about food?" he countered

I sighed. "Only a small bite, okay? Quick in and out," I told him, knowing for a fact I was fine, but I had to remember that the image of the cats was new for Kane. Maybe he just needed a moment to decompress.

"Don't worry, it'll be quick," he reassured.

I nodded and looked ahead. The restaurant was past the station, but I suppose it was still early enough, so it shouldn't be an issue. It was a little out of character for me, but I also had to consider Kane's needs instead of ignoring mine.

4

When we reached Johnson's, I parked close to the door since the only other vehicles were a light blue van and a black mini-car. Both were owned by the brothers running the restaurant.

Turning off the car, I hesitated momentarily before pulling the bag I had received from Poppy from my jacket. Then I leaned over to place the bag into the jockey box, bumping Kane's leg a little.

"Why are you putting that in there?" he asked, moving his leg out of the way.

"I don't really want to bring this stuff into the restaurant," I responded as I got out of the car, Kane following suit. My pocket felt less heavy, not that the small bag was heavy; it was more that I feared it would leak out. I know it was sealed in there well, but with an acid that strong, I wasn't planning on risking it.

Once we were situated, the both of us made our way to the front door, a small bell jingling above our heads.

The display in front of the door never disappoints as colorful cakes, cupcakes, and pies line inside with a register sitting on top. Along the walls are arctic blue booths with matching-colored chairs around the black tables.

A small shelf filled with all sorts of old car models lined the top of the walls.

Behind the display sat a black-style saloon door where I could see the kitchen, sounds of things moving around inside as if someone was cooking. However, I couldn't see anyone when I suddenly heard a small bell to my right. When I glanced down at the display, I saw Kane had pressed the small golden bell.

Immediately, a loud thump came from the saloon door as Mike

came out from the kitchen. His ice-blue eyes contrasted with his short blond hair. His neatly purple button-up shirt had a few red stains and flour powdered over his blue jeans.

"Oh hey, Mill!" he announced in his usual chirpy tone, leaning forward on the counter.

"Let me guess, you want a coffee and Kane our double deluxe pancakes?" Mike guessed.

"That sounds amazing!" Kane exclaimed, almost jumping with excitement.

"A coffee and your cheddar broccoli soup," I told him.

"Oh, changing it up a little, eh? You two go sit down. I'll get this ticket to Bob for your food and be right out with that coffee."

"Thank you," I told him, leading Kane to the left, taking the second booth so I could see out of the window overlooking the main road, letting myself get lost in thought.

I was curious to know where this whole mystery was leading the connections between Margy's cats, the critters, and Gary's. Then, those two hikers seemed wildly different.

I know it's still early in the case, so nothing will make sense, at least until we can get more information. Though this killer isn't leaving any trails, there are those acid... Pits? But I haven't noticed anything else that could help track down a specific person.

"What's the game plan?" Kane asked me

"It's hard to say. Whoever is spreading this acid must have a way of making it so they have enough space to do so safely. I personally don't know the process, but Poppy may have an answer."

Kane leaned back in the booth as if thinking something over. "Well, there is that new science teacher?" he suggested

"Besides just knowing Science, is there any reason we should put him on the list of suspects?" I asked him

"Oh, well, he did just move here pretty recently, a few weeks before the two hikers were found dead."

I tapped my chin, thinking it over. "Well, I suppose if Poppy doesn't have anything for me, I guess it wouldn't hurt to at least speak with him," I said, becoming startled when Mike suddenly appeared beside us at the table, placing a large blue rounded cup of chocolate milk in front of Kane as he put a smaller white cup in front of me with my coffee.

"I didn't order a drink," Kane told him.

"It's on the house; Bob will have your food out shortly," he told us, offering a warm smile.

"Oh, Thanks, Mike!" Kane responded as he started to sip on his chocolate milk

"I'm Looking forward to the food," I told him, picking up my dark coffee. The pungent smell hitting me before I even took a sip.

"Yeah, I'm headed out for the day, so he'll bring it out."

"Seems sorta early for you to head out," I comment.

"Oh well, Bob is the one who can cook. It's slow, and I got everything else done. I have a few things I need to take care of anyway."

"Well, thanks for bringing us our drinks. It was nice seeing you," I told him.

"you guys also, good luck with the case," he said, walking off before I could say anything else.

"He seemed to be in a hurry," Kane spoke.

"I suppose it might just be a busy day for him," I told him, sipping my coffee.

Silence formed between us, the soft music from the worn speakers helping fill it as some country song played; quiet moments like this remind me of why I left Northwood. I loved the people here, but the town is quiet and void of anything. I suppose that it would be unfair to say this town is what made me who I am. It's not exciting like the big city, but I do have plenty of fond memories of my childhood, and I should never forget that.

"HEY," a booming voice startled me, causing me to turn my bed and see Bob make his way to our table. He had greeted us all the way at the counter, his voice was so loud it sounded like it was right by me.

Bob is a tall bear of a man who looks very huggable, his short strawberry blond hair trapped in a hair net, with chocolate eyes bursting with kindness as he approached us with our food in both hands.

"Loud as ever," I told him.

"I don't plan to change it," Bob said, a smile across his lips as he placed a plate of pancakes in front of Kane and my soup in front of me. Knowing the both of us well enough, he didn't even have to ask what we had ordered.

"What are you doing here together?" Bob asked, looking between us. "This is the first time I've seen you eat out with anyone."

"He's helping me on a case," I informed Bob.

"The big-time detective has a partner? Never thought I would see the day," Bob teased.

"I'm a pretty good partner," Kane chimed in, mouth half full of pancakes

"You're doing well," I told him

Bob gave a hefty laugh. "Well, I think it's good for you, Mill, moping around everywhere. You need more interactions than with that cat of yours."

"Marshmallow is amazing company, and she's not very loud," I commented back, not entirely a fan of people telling me I need to get out more. I know what I like, and that's keeping to myself.

"Mill doesn't mope around," Kane told Bob. "he's just a quiet guy."

"Oh," Bob spoke, seeming to back off a little.

I was a little surprised by Kane's sudden defense of me. I don't entirely mind Bob's teasing, but I've also gotten so used to it that it was refreshing. Kane tried to put a stop to it.

"Have you two gotten any leads for the case?" Bob asked, changing the subject.

"Not yet," I told him, sighing softly. "We were discussing possible people, but we don't have enough clues."

Kane nodded. "Has anyone new come by to eat here?" he asked.

Bob paused momentarily, thinking, "Yeah, I had. Mike has been leaving early most days doing whatever the hell he's up to, so I've been dealing with customers more than usual," he started. "I don't know what Mike has been up to, but I've been getting left here a lot alone. It's not like we're busy normally. It's just a lot of work dealing with everything by myself."

"I'm sorry to hear" I spoke up.

"Mike has loved this place more than I did, so for him to suddenly be disappearing so much has been out of character."

"Well, I hope he's well," I said.

"You said you've been seeing new customers?" Kane asked, keeping the conversation on track

"oh yeah, there's this sweet lady with a baby that moved in, Sydney, I think, and Declan has been coming by almost every Friday. I heard He's replacing the science teacher in the school," Bob spoke, his eyes shifting between us as he spoke.

"Anything off about Declan?" Kane asked

"he's a weird guy, but honestly, I would say the same about Mill."

"Hey," I spoke up.

"He acts just like you," Bob remarked. "He keeps to himself and is a big coffee addict."

"Just that?" Kane asked

Bob nodded. "Just a keep-to-yourself person; a few others have filtered through, but not enough. I've gotten to know them."

"Thanks for all the helpful information," I said, a little bitter at his comments about me as I sipped my coffee.

"It's not a problem," Bob said, not seeming to catch my tone. "If you two need anything, just give a holler. I'm doing a deep clean in the back."

"Thank you, will do," I told him, watching him walk back behind the counter.

I glance down at my food. Kane had already eaten one of his pancakes; he wasn't kidding about being hungry.

I pick up my spoon and sip some of the soup, a smile forming on my lips, the warmth of it filling my soul. As I ate a few more bites, my eyes wandered over to Kane; his pancakes looked as if they had been inhaled.

"I may be overthinking this, but it's sort of weird for Mike to leave the restaurant," I comment.

"I suppose that was weird. I don't know Mike as well, but I don't recall the brothers not being together. However, it is slow. Maybe Mike just has more important things?"

I bit my lip. "You might be right, but it doesn't sit right in my gut. Bob said he still has trouble managing the place; I can't imagine Mike just leaving him high and dry."

"I'm sure he has his reasons," Kane spoke, finishing off his drink

I nodded, still finding it strange when my phone buzzed from within the jacket of my overcoat. I pulled it out, seeing it was from the Boss.

"Hello," I spoke.

"Hey, Mill, I have some good news. Poppy has found some information that would be helpful in your investigation. Would you be able to come to her office?"

"Oh yeah, definitely, Kane and I will be right over," I tell him, thankful for something to happen. I can always count on Poppy to find out information. She would be a fantastic detective, but she's pretty damn good at her current job.

"Alright, see you soon," Boss replied before I heard the phone click off, and I put it back into my pocket.

"What's up?" Kane asked, his plate and cup stacked on the edge of the table

"Poppy has information for us. We should head to the station," I tell him as I pull my wallet out and place money on the table, drinking the last of my coffee before getting up.

"Oh, I could help pay."

"It's fine, come on," I tell him. "I want to get to the station."

"Alright, I'm going," Kane responded as I walked to the front counter.

"Hey, Bob! Money's on the counter. I'll see you later," I called out

"Alright! You two have a safe trip," He responded, his voice booming from the kitchen.

Kane followed me out of the front door and to my car

"What sort of information do you think she has?" Kane asked, getting into the passenger seat

I groaned as I got into the driver's side. "Boss didn't mention anything, but I assume it's important, considering he called me personally."

"Well, I hope it gives us a good path to follow."

"Well, it really depends," I tell him as I pull onto the road and head to the station. "It may just lead us to smaller clues to follow, which don't always help, but in such a small town, it can make a world of difference," I told him.

Kane nodded as I drove us to the station. Once there, I parked near the front. Ensuring this, I grabbed the small bag with the acid sample from the jockey box and slipped it into my jacket. Exiting and headed into the station. Inside, the silence was crushing in the empty lobby, having a strange air about it as I turned to glance at the Boss's door. Seeing it closed, I wondered if he was there but could not see inside.

"Maybe Poppy is in her office?" Kane suggested

"Oh yeah, we can at least talk to her," I tell him. Walking forward to the doors, we make our way down to Poppy's office. Looking into the large window on the right wall, I saw her back facing us, so I pushed the door open to enter the table in the middle of the room, still covered in papers. At the same time, she seemed to be working on something I couldn't see.

"Poppy?" I asked, startling her as she dropped an empty vile, shattering it on the floor. "Oh no, I'm sorry," I apologized, not having meant to spook her.

"Oh, it's okay," she told me as she grabbed a hanging mini broom and dustpan and quickly swept it up. I get that you got the call from the Boss, then?" she asked me. Her wild red hair was restrained into a ponytail, her goggles around her neck, her nice white lab coat went down to her knees, a skirt showing from under it.

"Yeah, it's why we're here. The Boss said you had some important information?"

"Oh yes," she replied as she grabbed a small vile on the counter, returning to us. "This acid is unlike anything I had ever seen. The closest thing I could track it to is Fluoroantimonic acid, which is very acidic, but... I just can't figure out what else is in it. I've never seen an acid this powerful before. Even the vials I keep it in are slowly getting broken down.

"So this is Strong enough to break down organic and non-organic?" Kane asked

"Yes, I've been running tests, and it doesn't matter what I place inside. It will break it down; organic material breaks down much faster, while non-organic material takes its time, but even then, it's still broken down. It's fascinating!"

I looked between Poppy and Kane as their words blurred together. A sudden realization hit me, and I quickly dug into my jacket pocket, gasping when I pulled out the bag with the vials. A stinging sensation hit my hand, causing me to drop the bag on the table. The acid was slowly eating it away and was only seconds away from spilling into the pocket. Melted plastic stuck to my hand from where it was being eaten away.

"Are you okay?!" Kane asked, rushing to my side as he took my arm

"Yeah, I'm good. Got it out in time."

"I'm sorry, Mill, I should have warned you ahead of time," Poppy spoke as she took some tweezers and dropped the bag into a glass container to contain it.

"Did it burn you?" Kane asked

"A little," I told him, my left hand stinging

"Here," Poppy said, quickly dabbing the skin with a wet cloth and patting it dry. "These can be serious, Mill," she explained, placing a jelly substance over my palm and then a bandage. It needs to be washed daily and patted dry."

"Thank you," I told her, placing my right hand over the bandage. It stung a little less now.

"The sample is still useable, at least," Poppy said as she used tweezers to unfold the bag and pull the leaking vial out.

"How much would it take to make an acid like this?" Kane asked

"That's the thing," Poppy said, glancing between us. "I don't know how you can make acid with the right stuff, but. . . This stuff is nothing like I've ever seen before. The coloring, the texture, how it works and moves, it's almost like a living thing on its own."

"Are you saying this could be natural?" I asked her

"I don't know, either that or someone somehow created this stuff and is spreading it around Northwood for some godforsaken reason."

"It wouldn't make sense," Kane chimed in

"It could be a test to further their skills," I told him

"I'll go to the site myself to look for any signs of it forming naturally."

"Keep in close contact. We'll keep doing what we're doing," I told her

"You'll be the first one I call if I find anything odd," Poppy spoke, offering a soft smile. "now shoo, I got work to do, and I need silence,"

"Alright, good luck," I responded as we stepped out of the room. Poppy turned her back and went to work.

Alone in the hall, Kane and I exchanged glances before returning to the lobby.

Nothing noticeable had changed as I started back to the front doors. Glancing at the Boss's office, I hesitated, almost tripping over my feet when Kane grabbed my shoulder.

"You okay?" he asked.

"yeah, I just got distracted," I told him. Watching the office, the little screen was still shut, but I saw the light on and two silhouettes inside. The Boss, most likely, and was that Benny? It looked like a man, and it looked to be about Benny's height.

"Oh, the boss is in," Kane said

"yeah, but he's with Benny, I think. We talked with Poppy like we were supposed to. Let's go scout out the apartment building and let them work."

"Oh, you sure?"

I nodded. "yeah if he has anything for us, he can always call."

"Well, alright," he responded, following me to the front doors.

Once I get to my car, I plop down into the seat, shutting the door with a flinch, my hand stinging from gripping the door handle; I'll have to be more careful about that in the future.

My green eyes felt tired; glancing down at the ignition, I turned my key into it, hearing the hum of my vehicle come to life pull out of the parking lot.

"where are we headed to?" Kane asked

"Since the apartment building has some new people, we could talk to some of them and get a feel for what we are working with."

"Oh! I'm pretty excited to interview people," Kane admitted as he opened his window, letting the cool air fill the car.

"It's all part of being a detective."

"Well, I definitely feel like one now. I promise I'll be helpful."

"You are already helpful, Kane. Don't ever second guess yourself, okay?"

"How do I know my choices are right, though?"

I glanced at him, his milky brown eyes meeting mine as I quickly looked back to the road.

"Just feel your gut, okay? There may come a moment when you have to choose independently, and I may not be there to help guide you. Just remember who you are and follow what feels right."

"Have you ever been in those situations?" He asked

"Yeah, plenty of times, but I worked in the big city for a while. It was a lot more hectic."

"Have you ever shot anyone because of those situations?"

"Yes, but sometimes you have no choice," I replied.

"I'll try my best to make the right choices."

"I don't doubt it. You got a good head on your shoulders. I don't doubt you for a second," I told him; I could see him smile from the corner of my eye as I saw the apartment building coming up.

"You live here, don't you?" I asked him

"yeah, the third floor," he told me.

"I never thought they would make something like this," I told him, parking the car close to the entrance.

"I'm not; it was the perfect room for the taking."

"I suppose I just feel like this place is changing too fast."

"You sound old," Kane teased, getting out of the car.

I followed suit. "I'm not that much older than you," I scoffed back

"Come on, gramps," he teased further, leading me into the building.

Inside the claustrophobic lobby, emergency doors sit to our left; the floor is a cheap-looking dark wood that travels up the stairs, matching almost too closely. A pocket formed on the stairs where you turn around to keep going up.

"These are the mailboxes," Kane said as he gestured to the wall to the right of us. The mailboxes lined up with each apartment's number, but only a few had a first name printed on them.

I move over to the wall, looking over the different rooms.

320 for Zion, 410 for Sydney, 136 for Scott, 313 for Kane's name, and finally, 440 for Declan.

"I expected more people," I tell Kane as I pull out my notebook to write this all down.

"Well, it hasn't been up for too long, so maybe it just needs time?" he replied. "We could start on the fourth floor."

"Yeah, let's do that," I told him, figuring it wouldn't hurt. We could speak to the people here and get a sense of them.

Letting Kane walk ahead of me, we head up the stairs. The lack of an elevator was noticeable, which was strange. Aren't these sorts of places required to have one? If not for convenience but for anyone with a disability, especially since there were no first-floor rooms.

Our footsteps echoed through the apartment complex as we took the turn leading up higher to the first floor; the same wood followed us, but this time, a long dark blue rug or carpet? It lay in the hall but only in the middle, leaving the wood to show on the sides, looking like a massive tripping hazard.

Kane took the turn up to the other sets of stairs, and I followed as we made it to the second floor. The same dark blue carpet rug lay down the hall as I followed Kane further up.

Once we were on the third floor, Kane paused, causing me to run into him.

He stumbled forward, and I caught myself on the wall before I could entirely fall.

"Sorry," Kane said, turning to face me

"What happened?" I asked him

"I was thinking about what we were going to say when we started talking to people, and I guess I just got lost in thought."

"Oh, don't worry about that. I'll do the talking. You listen and learn, okay?"

"Oh yeah, I suppose that makes sense. You're the one with the experience here."

I nodded. "You'll get the hang of it, Kane, but this is your first official case, so just try and learn as much as you can for now, okay?"

"I'll suck up every bit of knowledge you are willing to share with me!" he spoke eagerly.

"Woah there, I can only teach you so much, okay? You gotta think on your own, too," I told him, starting back up the stairs.

"Don't worry, I'll do that too, but I'll still suck up any sort of knowledge you can share."

I rolled my eyes but smiled as we reached the fourth floor.

"So we're going to try speaking with everyone?" Kane asked, stepping beside me.

"That's the plan. We don't have any leads yet, and someone around here might have some new information for us," I explained. "It's not always a way we go. I honestly don't enjoy bothering people, but this keeps us busy, and something good might come out of it."

"so we are grasping at straws right now?" Kane asked

"I wouldn't put it that way, but yeah," I replied, pulling my small book out. "It looks like Declen is in room 440. Let's see if he's home and willing to answer a few questions," I told Kane, walking down the left of the hall.

"What if he refuses?" Kane asked.

"Then we leave him alone. He's not obligated to talk to us."

"Wouldn't that make him suspicious?"

"Not entirely; everyone has their rights, and I know it can be annoying to be bothered."

"Oh, I didn't think of that," Kane told me as he followed me to room 440.

"It's okay; you'll learn as we go," I told him, turning my attention to the door and knocking on it.

Waiting a few moments, I didn't hear anything, so I leaned in to see if I couldn't before raising my hand again.

"He's out," a feminine voice to my left. I turned to face her to see a woman stepping out from a door; she stood at about 5'6 with long red hair tied back with a blue ribbon and bright blue eyes. Freckles covered her cheeks, and she wore a yellow sun dress. A red baby stroller in front of her.

"Hello, ma'am," I spoke, stepping closer to her and noticing she stepped out of room 410. This must be Sydney.

"You must be Mill," she said.

"And you are Sydney, correct?" I asked

"That is me; if you're looking for Declan, I saw him leave an hour ago."

"Well, thank you. We're speaking with everyone around here. Do you have a second?"

"I suppose I do. Is this about that murder? I read it in the paper. I left the big city to escape stuff like that, but I guess it follows you everywhere."

"Yeah, unfortunately, things like this can happen even in a small town like this."

"I suppose I just want a safe place for my baby boy."

"What's his name?" Kane asked

"It's Elton," she replied, pulling the small cover back on the baby stroller to show a sleeping baby in a yellow onesie, his cheeks covered in freckles just like hers. "he's seven months old, and the big city was too much for us, so when I saw a room available in this apartment, I took it for a calmer life."

"It's just the two of you?" I asked her

She gave the nod. "his father was sick for a long time and passed before Elton was born."

"oh, I'm sorry," I apologized, not having meant to bring up a bad past.

"Don't be," she replied, offering a smile. "we knew it was going to happen. We just enjoyed the time we had together, and Elton was a little bit of a surprise. I wouldn't change anything; I do miss his father, but life will throw things at you, and all you can do is try to get by."

"That's a way to look at it," I told her

She nodded. "What questions did you have for me?" She asked

"Kane and I are just going around to see if anyone here has seen anything strange lately."

Sydney paused momentarily as if thinking, "I haven't been here long enough to really notice things, but I hear a lot of stories about the woods. What's about that? The people who've been here a long time act as if it's haunted."

"They're pretty thick, and it's easy to get lost. The older people around here are just very superstitious."

"That's it?" she asked.

"I think it's haunted' Kane spoke up. "my folks used to talk about weird creatures living in the woods."

"Or just wolves and coyotes," I spoke. "I suggest staying out of the woods regardless. We're still trying to figure out who is behind the murder case."

"Thank you. Was there anything else you wanted to ask?" she asked

"No, that's all I had for you," I told her

"Well, if you guys ever need to ask me anything else, you are welcome to stop by anytime. I can't promise I'll be home, but you can always try," she spoke with a soft laugh. "I'm taking Elton out for a stroll, so you two have a good day," she added, walking past us.

"You have a good day," I told her

"She was nice," Kane said

"Yeah, we could cross her off our suspicious list for now unless something leads to her."

"I don't think she has anything to do with it."

"I don't either. Unless something comes up, I'm just saying she's off the list."

"are we going to talk to anyone else?" Kane asked

"We can see if anyone else is home," I told him

"Alright, I think Zion is on the third floor."

"They really spread everyone out," I told him, heading back to the stairs and making our way back down to the third floor. Checking my phone, I head over to 320, making sure Kane is beside me. I lightly knocked on the door.

After only a moment, the door opened. A man with medium-length black hair and brown eyes stood there. He appeared a bit older than me, possibly in his thirties? he wore blue sweats and a long gray shirt.

"Are you the maintenance guy?" the man asked

"Is there something wrong with your apartment?" I asked him

"Yeah, the hot water isn't working. The landlord said he would send someone over."

"Oh, well, sorry to disappoint. I'm Mill, the detective of this town, and this is Kane, my partner."

"I take it this is about that case in the paper?"

"Yes, we are just going around to see if anyone has seen or heard anything weird."

"Hmm, nothing jumps out to me, Oh! But you guys should talk with Declan! he was over at the hardware shop where I just started and was talking about seeing weird things in the woods."

"Did he say what he saw?" I asked

"He didn't go into specifics. Maybe he was worried I would think he was weird."

"All right, well, thanks for your advice."

"Not a problem. Good luck to you two."

I tipped my hat to him as he closed the door, turning around to face the stairs.

"What's the plan now?" Kane asked

"I think there's one last person we can speak to, but talking with Declan might be worth it if he's seen something strange."

"I wonder what it is," Kane spoke.

"Hopefully, something helpful," I tell him, walking to the stairs and going to the first floor. The lobby still below us.

"Scott is in room 136," I spoke out loud, making my way to the door, a sign hanging on the knob saying 'Out.'

"I'm assuming this means he isn't home," I spoke

"I guess we won't get to talk to him either," Kane said

"It's okay," I told him, pulling my phone out. It was starting to get late. I guess all the running around to Margy's and coming here took longer than I thought,

"I need to get home to Marshmallow. It's her dinner time."

"oh yeah, you should get home then," Kane told me

"Why don't we plan to meet in the morning?" I suggest

"You'll call me when you get up?" He half asked

"Oh sure, I could do that."

"Yeah! I can't wait."

I rolled my eyes but smiled. "Get off to your place. I'll call you in the morning."

"Alright, I'll see you," Kane said, almost too cheery, as he descended the steps.

I rubbed my eyes. It didn't feel like a long day, but I was still tired. Maybe it just didn't feel that way because we ended up with no leads. Hopefully, we will have better luck tomorrow.

Knowing there was nothing else for me, I left the building to my car, sighing softly before getting into it.

Turning my key in its ignition, I paused momentarily, glancing down at my radio before turning it on to soft ambient music to help clear my mind.

Turning the car onto the main, I headed to my home. The drive was quiet besides the music as it helped clear my mind, the sun low in the sky, reflecting a golden glow over the trees.

If I remember correctly, my mom told me this was called the golden hour. She would spend this short period of time taking pictures of the trees and the occasional bird... She loved that camera.

Biting my lip hard, I tasted copper. I hated thinking of them and what could have been and what should have been. I miss them a lot and know nothing will bring them back.

I took a breath and turned on the road to my place, parking in front of the house.

After sitting there briefly, I finally turned off the car and got out. Everything seemed more or less normal here besides the giant blue mushroom in my yard close to the trees. I'm no mushroom expert, but this is the only place I've seen mushrooms that big and with odd coloring. I always figured it was just due to the environment.

I enter the house, stopping by the door to remove my Fedora and jacket before kicking off my shoes. All the while, a little bell moves down the hall, and soft meows fill the air.

"Hey there, Marsh," I say, looking down at her. She gives another meow, her little bell ringing as I scoop her into my arms and walk into the kitchen. She rubbed her head against my chin, tickling my nose with her long whiskers, so I placed her on the kitchen table so I could grab one of her canned foods.

Opening the drawer, I realized she only had enough for tonight's dinner and breakfast, so I'll have to stop by the shop early in the morning to ensure I get more.

Prying it open, I placed what I had into her bowl with a gross, squishy noise. Still, it seemed to please her as she quickly jumped down and ran to her food bowl to eat up what I put into it. I grabbed a muffin from the cabinet to eat, not really in the mood to do any sort of cooking,

I looked down at my Marshmallow as she ate. I'm glad she enjoyed it. I leave the kitchen and walk down the hall to my bedroom. I ate the muffin as I went, finishing my small meal quickly.

Looking around the room, I walked to the closet. I pulled out a red baggy shirt and gray pajama bottoms, swapping my clothing out into them, dropping my dirty clothing onto the floor to take care of in the morning... Or whenever I get to it.

Crawling into my bed tiredly, I laid my head on my feathered pillow, letting it consume me when a soft bell rang by the door until I felt something small jump onto the bed.

"Oh, you're such a good girl," I said as she curled beside me.

"Get some sleep, girl; tomorrow is going to be a long day," I added with a soft yawn as I closed my eyes and fell into a deep sleep.

5

I woke up the next day with a paw in my face and a loud meow. Opening my eyes, Marshmallow was trying to get my attention. "What is it, girl?" I groggily asked, but all I got in return was a long squeak of a meow.

"Okay, okay, I'm up," I tell her, sitting up. I did not even have a second to wake up before she smacked me in the face and then ran off, slipping through the door. Rubbing my cheek, "Good morning to you, too," I say, getting out of bed, knowing she was probably hungry. Looking around my nightstand, I realize I had left my phone in my jacket. Sighing, I grab my watch instead; seeing it's seven in the morning, I decide it is time to get up.

Standing up, I grab a bundle of clothing and then leave the room, hearing the faint meow of Marshmallow in the living room. I decide to leave her to her own devices as I go into the restroom; she can wait a few minutes.

The bathroom is a pretty decent size, with a large tub and shower to the far left corner, the sink to my right with drawers under it, while straight ahead of me from the door is the toilet, the walls are a red coloring with black tile along the bathtub wall.

I Placed my clothing on the closed toilet, then pulled my shirt off to a large bruise across my right shoulder; I don't remember getting this. The blue coloring showed how intense it was.

I turned to look at my back to examine the other bruise I'd had for a few days now; ever since I moved into this house, I kept waking up to new ones on random days. I don't know how or why. I've had Marshmallow for a while, so I knew she couldn't be causing this.

Biting my lip, I grabbed my fresh white shirt and pulled it over my head, then pulled up my jeans, taking a deep breath. The smell of old wood insulted my senses. This house could use a good deep cleaning, but I can only bring myself to do the bare minimum. My mother's shells still line around the sink's outer side, with one of my dad's old magazines on the toilet tank.

Everything here reminds me of them, I can't bear to get rid of anything.

A meow and scratching at the house brings me back to the present. I opened the door to look down at my white fluff ball. She gave me a squeak and ran off towards the kitchen.

"You act like I don't feed ya," I spoke, a smile crossing my lips as I stepped out, leaving my old clothing on the bathroom floor.

Before I could make my way to the kitchen, I caught a glimpse of the living room, spotting the glass sliding door cracked open again.

Feeling a thump of nerves strike my heart, I make my way over, quickly shutting it and replacing the wooden stick, hoping it'll stay.

Watching the dark woods for a moment, I felt like this place was haunted, which couldn't be true. The existence of ghosts was fake; it was probably just Marshmallow playing with it and somehow moving the stick which unlocked the door... Multiple times throughout the week.

Trying to convince myself this, I turned and walked to the kitchen, where she had tipped her food bowl over.

"Here." I took the last can of food from the drawer and filled the bowl with her food.

She went for it like a Piranha.

"Your welcome," I spoke, opening my fridge "Shit," I added, not feeling like food, so I just grabbed a pickle from the jar and started a pot of coffee.

I ate the pickle entirely before I knelt beside Marshmallow to give her a few pets while she finished her food, her fluffy tail swaying from side to side.

"Be a good girl while I'm gone, okay?" I told her as if she could understand me, and she gave me a meow when I scratched under her chin.

I wish I could stay here all day with her, but there's a case to solve. "I'll make sure to get your favorite treat," I told her, standing up. I grabbed a pink thermos from the cabinet and filled it with coffee.

With my morning coffee set and Marshmallow fed, I went to the front door. I grab my jacket, swapping my thermos from one hand to the other as I put it on, and then I slip my shoes on before I grab my Fedora.

Making one last glance behind me into the house, I could see Marshmallow watching me from around the corner.

"I'll be home soon," I told her, opening the door and walking out.

I had to let my eyes adjust to the dim light. The sun barely rose at this hour, and the porch was broken, so I carefully made my way across the wooden surface and somehow made it down the steps without an accident.

Reaching into my jacket, I pull out my keys before I sit in my car so I can immediately start it up and set my thermos into its cup holder. The headlights turn on, illuminating my front door and part of my yard; that spot where I had seen the blue mushroom just the night before, I realized, is gone; could I have just been mistaken? I remember clearly seeing it out here.

I pinch the bridge of my nose, taking a deep breath. I must be more tired than I thought. After this case, I am going to drive to some hot springs and just relax, or maybe I'll just run a hot bath at home. It would be closer to Marshmallow unless hot springs accept cats? I doubt that, though, so I'll settle for a bath and some coffee.

For now, I need to run to the store and get some groceries. I can worry about fungi when I don't have so much on my plate. I back out of my driveway and head onto the main road, taking the right turn to head into town.

I cruised past the police station and the small downtown area. I went to the grocery store, a long building with a massive sign saying NorthWood Grocers. It's the only place in town to get groceries besides the small shop downtown, but it doesn't carry much.

I do miss the different types of coffees I used to buy back in Saint Paul, not that Northwood doesn't have a small selection. The city just had so many more, and it was fun to try them all.

I park in the small lot only a few yards from the door, shutting it off and stepping out. I plan to make this trip quick. I need cat food, some more coffee and a few food items for myself. With that in mind, I walk up to the front doors and they slide open for me to step inside easily.

Four cash registers line up close to the right side. As I walk past them from the left, I don't see anyone yet. Still, if I remember correctly, Debbie, the store manager, and Nora were the only employees working there. It didn't get busy often, so I guess they didn't need much help, but I can imagine you would want at least a larger team even here. Hopefully as more people move in they will get more hires.

Even though we were in a small town, the store looked exactly like any other store. You would walk into the blaring lights above, the white walls and countless shelves.

I come here fairly often so I quickly walked around the shelves, wishing I had grabbed a cart or basket because my hands were filled with canned cat food and a new mouse toy. After all, she deserves it. Then I headed to the far back and grabbed some premade sandwiches out of the little cold area to help me through the next few days before I headed to one of the middle aisles to grab a coffee.

The selection is small, but I see my favorite brand, Draco. It's pretty good stuff. I bag up my favorite flavor. It is a smooth, dark roast. My attention going to a new flavor. They had something with caramel? That might be interesting. Completely lost in the world of coffee, I didn't notice the footsteps until a woman spoke, startling me as I dropped the bag of coffee to the floor and almost dropping the cans of food I got for Marshmallow. Whipping my head to the right, I see Debbie. She looked at me with expecting green eyes as if she had asked me a question, her dull brown hair cut short.

"Uhh, hi?" I spoke

"You didn't hear what I said, did you?" she questioned

"No," I admitted, "I honestly didn't hear you even walk up."

"Some detective you are; I asked how your kitty is doing."

"oh, she's pretty good; I'm getting her a mouse," I told her, showing the little mouse toy in the package.

"You spoil that poor cat."

"Well, she deserves it," I huffed. I was not too fond of it when others told me that. She was abandoned as a kitten. Of course, I spoil her. She deserves the world.

Debbie gave a bit of a chuckle as she picked up the coffee bag I had dropped. She stood shorter than me, reaching just barely to my chest. Her black polo had a name tag with Betty on it, a hell of a misspelling, and a black skirt matching the outfit.

"I could have picked that up," I told her.

"It's okay; I'm the one who spooked you," she said. Offering it to me. I awkwardly took it. I didn't want to buy this specific coffee, but I felt too awkward to put it back on the shelf after she picked it up.

"Say, Mill," Debbie spoke.

"Hmm?" I turn back to face her, hoping I could scurry away and escape.

"Have you gotten any clue on that case?"

"The couple at the park?" I clarified

"Of course, there isn't anything else going on in this place."

"I haven't gotten a lot," I told her.

"Oh, I thought you would have found something by now." Something about how she said that sent a shiver up my spine.

"Why is that?" I questioned

"Well, you're the best detective around, so I would naturally expect you to pick up on something."

"Please stop saying that; I'm just a normal detective. I'll find out who did it. You don't need to worry." I reassured her, though something kept nagging at me, that she wasn't worried about the murderer. In fact, her face looked pretty non expressive, making it hard to get an accurate reading of how she felt.

"Oh good," she replied finally, showing a smile that just felt unnatural. Did her smile always look like that?

"Thanks. . . Hey I gotta get going, I'll see you later," I spoke, stepping away. My nerves are getting the better of me and I need some air.

"Have a good day," she replied, walking down the aisle.

I let out a breath of air as I walked to the front cash register, finding Nora standing at the first one. She's a pretty lovely girl, a few years younger than me. I mostly know her from dating her older brother back in school before he went missing; that feels like such a long time ago.

She has medium-length blue hair and brown eyes, a long red feather placed behind her left ear, and is wearing the same uniform as Debbie but with black shorts instead of a skirt.

"Hey, Milly," Nora smirked, seeing me approach.

"I told you not to call me that, "I rolled my eyes. It's some stupid nickname that started when they wrote my name wrong in the yearbook forever in the text as a joke I can't seem to escape.

She snickered. "I'm just playing; I don't get to tease you much anymore, so I have to get it out of the way whenever I see you."

"Fine, I'll let it slide," I tell her. Silence fell between us as she scanned my items, pausing a moment before she could finish.

"Hey, Mill," she suddenly said

"Yeah?" I asked, looking her way, but she didn't meet my eyes, fixated on the can of cat food in her hand. "You okay?"

"I haven't been sleeping all too well," she told me

"Is something going on?" I questioned.

She looked around the space before leaning forward, signaling me to do the same, so I leaned forward, the scent of lavender hitting me as she whispered into my ear.

"I know who one of the killers is."

I jolt back, staring at her, failing to see some resemblance of a joke, but she had the most stern-faced I've ever seen her have

"I'm not fucking with you, Mill."

"If you know, why don't you call the station?"

"I think someone at the station is working with him."

"That's a huge accusation, Nora."

"That's why I've been so hesitant to tell anyone, but you are the only one I can trust; please just listen."

I reach into my jacket and pull out my notepad. "Okay, tell me everything you know," I tell her.

"Well..."she never got a word out as Debbie came out of nowhere. "What's going on over here?" Debbie asked.

Nora started to scan my items quickly but suddenly went quiet, so I turned to Debbie. Something was off here, and I needed answers from Nora.

"I'm going to step out with Nora for a second," I tell Debbie

"Well, whatever you two talk about, can't I be here for it, too?"

"It's personal business, Debbie," I spoke. Nora finished scanning my things, so I gave her my card, collected my bag, and took my card back.

"I'll be right back with her," I added. A part of my job is making sure the person I question feels safe, and Nora obviously did not feel comfortable with Debbie around.

We went outside the store and into the parking lot. Nora faces me towards the store, my back to it.

"This is pretty serious, Nora, so you better explain yourself clearly," I warned, not taking an accusation like this lightly.

She took a deep breath, seeming calmer now that it was the two of us. "I know I should have come to you sooner, but I just had to get my thoughts together. Then you showed up today, so it was perfect to let it out finally."

"Just tell me, Nora' I tell her, feeling impatient for what she has to say.

Nora nodded. "I've been going to the bar that Wallace owns since he lets me sit in the booths and do my homework in silence as long as I buy soda. And last night, while I was sitting in the far back, I felt someone sit behind me. When I turned around, I saw John and Debbie."

"Well, that's not really unusual, is it?" I questioned her; the two were close in age. John is a well-known cattle farmer. His place is a few miles down the main road out of Northwood. He has a lot of land.

"I didn't think so either until they started to whisper, maybe to keep me from hearing, but they sat right behind me, My back facing them, so I didn't exactly see their faces, but I recognized the voices."

I urged her to keep talking.

"I heard John tell Debbie that the job was done. Maybe he did some work for her, but then she spoke..." Nora paused, focusing on the store as if expecting something to come out at her.

"Debbie told him that the next target is bound to cause some stir in the town. And this is what freaked me out. John told Debbie that they have Benny in position," she paused, taking a deep breath. "I panicked, Mill. I gathered my things and ran. I don't know why it freaked me out so much. I should have been calmer, but I'm sure they noticed me scurry out like a fox. I sat by my phone last night trying to call you up, but I kept thinking, am I crazy? I wasn't sure, so I let myself think it over, and when I saw you, well... I just wanted to get it off my chest."

"If you hear things suspicious, call me any day or night, okay?" I told her, flipping my notepad closed, having written nothing since I held my groceries in my hand, but I'll remember.

"Do you feel like you are in danger?" I asked her

"No. . at least I hope not. I was pretty spooked, but I should be okay."

I nodded but read her face; she looked pretty uneasy. "I could have

Ryker keep an eye on your place?" I suggested

"I can't trust any of them, Mill... I only trust you. I'll be fine, really. I'll call you at the first sign of danger."

Against my better judgment, I bit my cheek. "Okay, do not hesitate to call me, okay? I'll take a look at what you told me. Thank you for the information." if what she says is true, it can cause a big problem in this town. I need to tread lightly and connect back with Kane. I'll think better once I drink some of the coffee I had left in the car.

"Thank you, Mill. I knew I could trust you. I should get back inside," she said, stepping backward.

"Don't tell anyone else about this, okay? Keep it between us."

"Don't worry, my lips are sealed," she replied, walking back into the store.

I stood in the parking lot for a few minutes, considering everything she had just told me. I wish she had come to me sooner, but I have it now; if this is a bigger ordeal than we had initially expected, we may need to call the police from outside of town if one of us, our own, is helping pull the strings. This will be a touchy subject, and if it's genuinely hazardous, I'll meet back up with Kane and see where we can go from there.

Sighing, my head ached, so I went to my car, slumping into the driver's seat and dropping the bag of cat food and unwanted coffee into my passenger seat. The sandwiches were getting smushed a little, and instead of fixing them, I grabbed my thermos, chugging down half the coffee.

My stomach didn't feel so good after I chugged that coffee. I should have had a larger dinner, so I grabbed one of my smushed sandwiched and ate a small portion to help settle my stomach.

Feeling better, I straighten up, turning on my car. I pulled out to head across the street to meet up with Kane.

I've never had trouble with a case like this before. Still, I guess being so close to these people makes it hard for me to imagine any of them scheming and planning to harm anyone; back in the big city, I just had Marshmallow, so it was easy to see anyone as a suspect.

Parking my car a few spots from the front door of the apartment complex, I step out of my vehicle, my eyes lingering on the sandwiches sitting in my seat; when will I be home? I wondered, not having thought this through, maybe they'll stay cool enough, so I shut the door, letting myself worry about this later, when I suddenly heard my name get shouted.

"huh?" was all I could get out before I was tackled into the pavement of the parking lot. The wind was knocked from me, but still, my hands gripped the person's shirt as I forced us over, pinning him down with a hand to his shoulder and shoving him down with my left hand, immediately going to my gun in its holster. Still, I stopped when I saw his face.

"Luke?!" I snarled, shoving his face into the concrete. "I could have hurt you!"

"You sorta hurting me now," He grumbled, his cheek scraped by the pavement, so I got off him and pulled him up.

"Damn, when did you get so quick?" Luke asked, rubbing his cheek

"I work alongside police. I've tackled plenty of people stronger than you."

"Aren't you just a detective? Soft and squishy," he joked, jabbing my rib, causing me to recoil back.

"I am, but sometimes I get wrapped up in the action."

"Well, I'll be more careful," he said

"Sorry about your cheek. Does it hurt?" I asked, feeling a twinge of guilt, but not much. He was the ass for tackling me.

"It'll be fine," he said, giving me a light push on the shoulder. "hey, we should go out for a drink," Luke suggested

"How about some other time? Kane's waiting for me."

"Kane? Oh, that short dude he could come to?"

"Luke, I'm working. I already spent a lot of time shopping."

Luke sighed. "You so much like your dad, you know that? Fine, how about this: if you find some time, drop by tonight at Wallace's bar?"

"I don't drink," I reminded him

"I'll make sure he has coffee."

I pinch the bridge of my nose, trying to focus for a moment, still a little annoyed that he thought it was appropriate to tackle me, but I suppose that's Luke for you. Ever since we were kids, he thought pushing James and me to our limits was funny, always dragging us off onto some fine adventure only to get us into trouble. To be fair, I went along with them, but it was Lucas who always instigated it.

"I'll consider it, now shoo. I gotta work," I spoke, waving him off like a puppy that was too needy.

"Fine, fine. Get to your work. I'll just sit alone waiting for you to arrive," he said dramatically.

I rolled my eyes. "Have fun," I replied, unable to help but smile as I turned to the building. Lucas laughed as I heard him walk off, too.

I finally entered the apartment complex, heading to the third floor to room 313. It felt a little strange walking up here. Maybe it's due to how little I still knew about Kane or the fact it's been ages since I've had a partner I didn't mind having around.

After my last one abandoned me, I hesitated to trust anyone again, but I weirdly felt like I could trust Kane.

I lifted my hand to knock on the door, but it swung open before I could even make contact. Kane stood in a baggy gray sweater with an elk on it and black sweats, his air a mess like he had just woken up;

seeing him in such casual clothing was strange. He almost looked entirely different without his ironed-out button-up shirt and perfectly fitting jeans.

"Your late" was the first word that came out of his mouth

"You don't look very ready," I commented back

"I was waiting for your call and got caught up in my book," he replied,

pausing. "Wait, how did you know I was about to knock?"

"You have heavy footsteps," he commented.

"Oh," was all I said. Did he recognize the sound of my steps to know I was coming?

He stepped aside to let me into the room. "There's fresh coffee," he told me as if it would lure me in. . . Well, it did.

I stepped into his small apartment room. The living room looked pretty ordinary. A couch sat in the middle, facing the left wall, where a TV stand and one of those large square TVs stood on top, the one that takes every ounce of strength within your being just to shift.

The kitchen was to the right. The sandy-colored carpet merged into white kitchen tile, where he had a small counter space with a white fridge filled with pictures of his family. It was hard to tell from where. There are cabinets over countertops and a messy stove. A coffee pot sat out on the counter by the fridge as it was about done brewing. Three doors line the back wall with a single poster by the first door of some game with a dragon and wizard? I don't play games.

"It's cozy," I told him

"take a seat. I'll bring you a coffee."

"I don't really have time to sit," I told him as he stepped over, a red mug already in hand, and handed it over to me.

"what do you mean?" He asked

"I spoke with Nora," I started but stopped when my phone started to buzz; handing the mug back over to Kane, I pulled it out to see it was Scarlet, so I quickly answered and brought it to my ear.

"Mill! There was a call; I need you at Nora's now," she quickly said, her voice labored.

"What's going on?" I asked, my stomach twisting into knots. She was just at the store a few minutes ago.

"She had placed a 911 call just a moment ago, and when Ryker and I showed up... Mill, it's bad, we need you to go there before..."

"Before what?"

"Before the acid completely eats everything away, I suggested leaving Kane. He won't be able to stomach it. I'm sorry, but please, you need to go now."

"I'll be there, "I told her, hanging up. My eyes lingered on the phone for a moment before putting it away and looking at Kane, who stared back with those wide brown eyes.

"Nora was found... I need to get to her place," I told him

"Oh, let me go throw on something."

"Kane, wait," I said, grabbing his arm before he could go. He looked back at me curiously.

"Scarlet told me you shouldn't go. It's. . . Bad."

He ripped his arm out from my grip. "I can't learn unless I stay by your side, Mill. Please, I will only be a minute; let me come."

I took a deep breath, concerned I didn't want to stand here and argue. "Fine, but you do what I say, okay?" I told him, and he gave me a nod before turning and disappearing into the middle room.

I pinched the bridge of my nose. I should have taken her more seriously right then and there, but how did she end up so soon at her place dead? If I hadn't been stopped by Luke, I wouldn't have ended up in the parking lot for so long...

Don't blame anyone. There was no way you could have known something like this would happen. I'll have to call Scarlet back once I'm in the car and tell her what Nora told me.

I turn back to Kane's room, hearing something clatter to the floor.

This is going to be a long hell of a day.

6

When Kane was finally ready, he came out in black dress pants and a messy blue buttoned-up shirt, half of which had been tucked into his pants. His socks were mismatched, white and black, and his hair was slightly disheveled from throwing on his shirt.

"ready?" I asked but was already making my way to the door, swinging it open, and he followed behind, clumsily getting his shoes on.

I quickly descended the stairs, stumbling once or twice, wanting to ensure we arrived as soon as possible. Kane did get ready pretty fast, but we could not waste a second.

I shoved the front doors only to get stopped in my tracks, groaning

"They're pull," Kane said, pulling one open to let me through, my shoulder aching.

"I forgot," I admitted as I finally reached my car. Kane got into the passenger seat after he had moved my bag of food and set it in the back.

Turning the key in the ignition, I switched gears and sped onto the main road, heading toward the station. I turn onto a road just before getting there that leads to the small neighborhood with houses of all shapes and sizes, most of them built by older residents over time and left either for their families or newcomers.

"Do you remember where her house is?" Kane asked

"Yeah, I've been there a few times," I replied, driving down the road, houses on either side of us as we reached the sixth one on the left, a one-story home with a warm pink and a black roof, her white car parked up front and the gate in front of her house is busted including the blue door. It looks like someone forced their way inside.

"Make sure you have your gun," I told him, pulling my gun out from the middle console and then slipping out of the car, surprised to not see Scarlet. I wondered if she was handling other things. Oh shit. . I forgot to call her . .

I'll have to do that later. Right now I need to get into the house and assist with the situation. She made it seem pretty vital. I hurried, so that's what I did.

I stepped over the rock path that led to the front door. Kane's footsteps were right behind me as we both kept utterly silent. I don't know why, but it felt right to make no noise until we reached the door.

The hinges on the top are destroyed, while the bottom ones are hanging by a single nail. Whoever did this was either very strong or had something to bring it down; my heart thumped. How could this all happen so fast? The timing of it all seemed so unreal.

I gave Kane a glance as he stood behind me. I didn't want to scare him if this was as bad as Scarlet had said. "You don't. ." he cut me off.

"Let's go," He spoke.

I only nodded. I suppose he'll see something awful at one point; I just hope it doesn't make him quit. I've seen a lot of confident people just up and leave.

I shouldn't be thinking of all of this. I focused my eyes on the hall leading into Nora's home. It led to the right, and I could see into a little of her living room with a door to the end on the left, the kitchen, I presume.

An odd but familiar smell filled the air the closer I got to the living room, like a rotting corpse, but that wouldn't make any sense. There's no way a body could rot so quickly. I glance back at Kane, who stands in the doorway waiting for me to move forward, so that's what I do, and slowly. I don't know why it just felt right at this moment. A heavy air flowed past me as if trying to stop me from seeing what was ahead, but I know this smell, it's the smell of death.

The smell grew stronger as I reached the door beside the kitchen, the living room opening to my right. The first thing coming to view was a large blue sofa with a flat-screen TV sitting on an entertainment center.

At first, I didn't see anything out of the ordinary. The smell suffocated me, making it hard to tell where it was coming from. So I took a few steps closer, and that's when I saw it.

A pool of blood came from around the couch, so I walked around to find where Nora was; she lay on her back, her head towards me, the coffee table leaning oddly away, one of its legs broken, and the corner closer to me was chipped. The items that were once on it were scattered.

There was a struggle, but it didn't look like much; either it was a surprise, or the intruder was strong.

I knelt down beside her, the rotting smell almost knocking me back. god, how could she be rotting already?

I heard Kane say something, but it was muffled. I whipped my head around just in time to see him disappear around the corner and then throw up. I was afraid of this, but I turned back to Nora. I'll console him after I'm done.

She wore clothing still, her head split open, and that's where the blood was coming from. My eyes turned back to the coffee table; I bet she was rammed into that, which was probably the hit that killed her. It must have been a sneak attack. It was the only thing damaged in this room.

I look down at her shirt, noticing a line from the top to the bottom starting to soak up a liquid, blood. I assumed that she was bleeding along the stomach and chest areas, so I reached into my inside pocket, searching for a moment until I pulled out a little metal rod that I stretched out.

I use it to prevent using my hands as I slip the end under the bottom of her shirt.

"Sorry, Nora," I whispered as I pulled her shirt up over her bra to see she had a cut that started from the breastbone down just below her belly button that appeared to have been sewn together? Blood seeping through in between the stitches.

Why would they cut her open like this? They should have known they had limited time. .Wait if she was knocked out, how could she have made that phone call? I looked around the area but couldn't see her phone in sight; she couldn't have survived being cut open like this. The hit to the head was probably enough to take her out, so when did she call?

Scarlet didn't mention any of these strange wounds, so she may have just seen Nora's cracked skull and assumed I should come to look, so I took the little metal rod and gently pressed it against her breastbone where the stitches were the rotting smell was definitely coming from inside her the smell seeming to grow more intense as a few of the stitches came loose effortlessly, it was a pretty sloppy job which meant they were in a hurry.

Pushing a little more, the sound of her sticky flesh came apart, the stitches unraveling, the smell punching me in the face as I brought my right arm up to cover my mouth and nose to prevent myself from gagging. I've never seen anything like this. . Where her organs are supposed to be there was nothing. Her insides dissolved as if acid was dumped into her cavity, and then she was sewn up.

"What did they do to you?" I asked, my voice muffled against my arm.

I didn't know how I should feel. Disgust is one feeling, but the shock is mostly what I felt. I stand up fully, stepping back a little to allow myself to breathe. I really hoped she was gone by the time they cut her open. My eyes trailed to my hand. The little bit of acid that got on my hand hurt like hell. The pain had subsided for the most part, but to have this stuff poured into you like this. . . I really hope the head injury is what took her out.

I glance around the room and walk back towards the kitchen, following the hall further down to find her bedroom and bathroom. Peeking into the bathroom, nothing seemed out of the ordinary; even the medicine cabinet above her white sink seemed pretty untouched. So I back out and walk into her very dark room. I turn on the light, taxidermy animals and quilts line the walls. It looked like a mess, but by the dirty clothing, I had a feeling it'd been like this, so I shut the light off and walked out.

I suppose they did this not to steal, though I may have already known that. Walking to the kitchen, I peek inside, the red walls untouched and the table a cluttered mess. It looks like Nora was working on another taxidermy animal, a rabbit. So she made those herself? Again, it's a mess but a very organized mess.

Stepping back from the kitchen I glance toward the couch. I need to call Scarlet and find out when Nora had called. None of this makes sense, so I walk back down the hall to the front door. I find Kane sitting on the steps, so I sit beside him.

"I'm sorry," Kane spoke.

"Don't be sorry, Kane. It's one thing seeing a body, another when it's someone you know."

"Does it ever get easier?"

"Not really, you just become numb to it."

Kane nodded. "I'll try and do better next time."

I put a hand on his shoulder. "I threw up the first time I saw a body, too, okay? We'll take things slowly. Don't force yourself."

"Thanks, Mill," Kane spoke, offering me a smile

"I need to call Scarlet. You stay right here, okay?" I told him, standing up and walking a few steps forward.

Digging into my pocket, I pull out my almost-dead phone. I should really charge this thing, but for now, I dial Scarlet, putting the phone up to my ear. After a few rings, she picked up.

"Hey, Scar..." I didn't even get a word out

"Mill! Thank goodness I was just about to call you. Need to get your ass up to Margy's now."

"Huh? What happened?" I asked

"James found her dead. It could be another murder, but we need you to get there and confirm it."

"Fuck" I muttered, glancing at Kane, who was watching me now. "Okay, we'll head right there. Can you get Poppy here to Nora's?"

"Yeah, we'll handle Nora. I'll talk to you later about what you found, but you need to hurry. They used the same tactic, and the acid will have her consumed before we can get any more evidence. James found her outside in the yard."

"we're going now," I informed her, hanging up.

"Is something wrong?" Kane asked, walking over to me.

"We need to get to Margy's. James found her. . . She's dead too," I informed him.

"What?" He gasped with shock

"Come on, Scarlet is going to send Poppy here. We need to rush up to Margy's now," I told him, jogging to my vehicle.

"This town is going crazy!" Kane said beside me as he followed.

"Yeah, I suppose you could say that," I tell him, slipping into the driver's seat, Kane in the passenger as always.

Starting the car, I was quick to drive back onto the road and head out of the neighborhood towards Margy's

"Who do you think did this?" Kane asked

"Well, when I spoke to Nora, she had suspected Debbie and John, but I haven't had a second to even try and look into it due to Nora and now Margy's death."

"Should I call Scarlet?" Kane asked

I hesitated, " There was a possibility of an officer also being involved, but if Nora was right, it could mean anyone at the station could be involved, so reporting it could cause a chain reaction."

"That's scary," Kane said

"I just need time to think it over, but there is so much happening I haven't been able to even think about it."

"Well, after we figure out what happened to Margy, I could help?" Kane offered

"Thanks, I might take you up on that," I told him. My mind was still reeling from everything that had happened today. It was too much, and I needed to clear my mind, but between Nora and Margy, I don't think that'll happen.

The car fell silent as I sped to Margy's place, wanting to get there quickly but still being careful of any wildlife. As we made it to her place, I pulled up and parked at the front of the house.

"Keep an eye out," I tell Kane as I leave the car, Kane following suit.

A few cats rushed through the tall grass before us, probably startled by the car doors slamming shut.

"Do we know where she is?" Kane asked

"Scarlet said James found her out in the yard," I tell him, stepping into the tall grass and walking steadily. I really hope she's not where I suspected she would be. . .

We make our way through the yard, the familiar smell of rotting flesh insulting my senses. But I keep reaching the same puddle of acid I encountered last time I was here, though this time instead of cats. Margy lies face down in it.

The sight made me sick to my stomach. Kane threw up behind me as I clenched my stomach to keep my composure.

Her skull is cracked open with brain matter seeping out of it, her body having been eaten away. Hence, her intestines and other organs lay sprawled out around her. Some are entirely gone, while some are partly dissolved, like some sick display.

I wonder if she had come out here to retrieve the cats. I know she was ill, but I don't think she would have been sick enough to try to retrieve her dead cats.

I should have had someone watching her or, at the very least, made sure James got here sooner. I couldn't imagine the guilt he must be facing.

I circled around the puddle, looking for anything out of the ordinary, when my eyes caught sight of a trail of strange black gelatinous material. It looked just like the acid but thicker, as if it had hardened. Dead grass formed around the hardened gelatinous acid.

I did not remember this, having been here. It stayed in the form of a ball and was placed a few feet away from each other, so I started to follow the ball's dead grass around each one, with a few dead, small critters here and there, as I reached the edge of the forest where the trail just ends cold.

Staring out into the woods, all I could see was the thick flora, the trees intertwining together as tall plants of various species spread all over.

Scanning the area, I carefully stepped forward. A pounding suddenly formed in my head, and my skin felt as if it was covered in spider webs, so I took a few steps back, instantly feeling better.

That was weird. It was like walking past a doorway.

Wanting to test this theory, I stepped forward again into the woods, the headache forming and the strange spiderweb feeling returning, so I backpedaled, instantly feeling better. This made no sense. Why did I feel so odd stepping into the woods? I looked around, but it all looked normal.

I turned away from the woods to face the house. I should have connected back with Kane, but I only got one step forward when I heard it.

A soft melody echoed from the woods, played off a bagpipe. The hauntingly beautiful sound filled me with a sudden sorrow, forcing me to face the woods and beckoning me forward.

I knew this was an awful idea. I needed to report what I saw and the trail. Still, the music rang in my ears like a siren call, and I stepped forward into the woods, ignoring the aching that formed and the spiderweb effect along my skin.

Walking through the woods, my pants protecting my legs from the tall plants. The headache and spiderweb effect slowly faded away the further I went. The music grew louder and almost moister as if the instrument had been dunked into water.

I still followed it, trudging through the woods, when a gush of wind blew through the woods, the trees rustling, and I gripped my fedora so it wouldn't fly off, the music suddenly stopping. I stood in the woods alone. The only sounds were critters in trees and my breathing. The wind had stopped altogether, just like the music.

Turning, I realized I didn't recognize anything. The trees looked different, almost as if they had all shifted, making me feel distraught.

I don't think I've walked in that deep, did I? That music... I couldn't stop myself. I felt so drawn to it. I took a few unsteady breaths and started walking forward, hoping it was the correct way, trying to recognize something, anything!

Another gust of wind forced its way through the thick trees, my fedora catching wind, causing me to snatch up to grab it. Turning around, I suddenly faced a massive field full of flowers.

"Where did this come from?" I mumbled.

Putting a foot forward, I step into the large field; it would have been impossible to overlook something like this; did I black out while walking? I looked down at my left hand. The burn hadn't been bothering me as bad as I pressed my right hand into it, nothing, so I pinched my arm, flinching. Alright, well, I'm awake.

A noise from behind drew my attention. It sounded like a deer in distress, so I turned, seeing nothing but trees. The deer didn't sound far away, so I stepped back into the thick trees towards the sound.

The ground was moist beneath my shoes, soaking them and the lower parts of my pant legs as I walked through damp grass. I stepped over a large root, noticing a large dead patch of grass. I took a few more steps to see the unholy sight.

The deer lay in a puddle of acid, making a distressing noise. However, how it's alive, I don't know; its head lay just outside of the acid while its lower body was being dissolved away, its stomach cavity split open. Its guts spilled out its legs against the ground were nothing but bone.

I held my stomach and turned away from it, vomiting onto the ground. Things don't usually get to me, but this made me sick as I wiped my mouth with a groan. Feeling sicker, I reached for my holstered gun.

This poor creature shouldn't be forced to suffer like this, so I take my gun and aim it at the creature's head. Taking a shot, it punctured through its skull, and the deer's head dropped. The deer was finally at peace... I hope.

Looking down at the deer, I holstered my gun back into place with shaking hands. I didn't understand what was happening, but I prayed Margy and the others didn't meet a fate like this deer. The thought of them suffering so slowly while their body was eaten away made me feel disgusted.

I turned away from the deer. The sight of it made my stomach turn. I closed my eyes to try and get some sort of sense back into me when I heard someone call my name.

I snapped my eyes open wide. It sounded like Kane. I quickly took in my surroundings, but I couldn't see him.

"Kane!" I called out

"Mill!" he responded from my right, so I turned and ran that way, my shoes slipping a little as I struggled against the wet ground, which quickly turned to mud. A large lake came into view.

"Kane!" I shouted out, spinning around, trying to find him

"Mill!" he responded, but I heard his voice from the lake.

"Kane...? "I asked, unsure. Scanning the water, I couldn't see anything; it was still, and his voice was so clear.

"Mill!" the voice again, this time distorted, like something trying to mimic Kane's voice.

I walk up to the lake, my reflection perfect as if I was looking into a mirror, a leaf falling beside the image rippling the water, my reflection's eyes quickly shift into a glowing red as my image turned into a shadow of a man, a heat emerging from the water as it bubbled and steamed.

I gasp and fall back, falling onto my ass, my face flushed from the intense heat of the water.

The water bubbled and rose as it formed into a person standing before me, heat radiating from it, making it hard to breathe as a cacophony of screams came from it; women and men of all ages erupted, making my ears ring.

Red glowing eyes shone through the water as it reached a hand out towards me.

Before the damn thing could even try to speak among the screams or reach out for me, I noped out of there, jumping to my feet and sprinting away. I am not dealing with this bullshit. I don't care if I'm high on some shroom or I'm out cold; I do not socialize with things that rise out of the water screaming.

I ran recklessly through the woods, branches smacking me in the face, rocks and roots making me stumble until one particular root snagged my shoe just right, causing me to face plant into the ground, my knees scraping against rocks and the wind being knocked out of me.

I closed my eyes for a moment to let my body recover, and once I felt okay, I groaned, standing up; the knees in my pants ripped up and bloodied, and a wetness on my right cheek formed as I wiped it, finding blood on my thumb and a cut across my cheek too.

I look down at my fedora on the ground, so I lean down, gripping it, and securely place it back onto my head when something bright reflects into my eyes. As I take a few steps forward, I spot Margy's house, the sun hitting a window just right to help guide me out of the woods.

I was never happier to see this place as I dropped to my sore knees. Exhaustion hit me like a ton of bricks.

"Mill!" Kane's voice rang out. I turned my head toward the sound, barely able to hear him over the pounding in my chest at the thought of that water monster. Still, when I saw Kane running my way from the house, I felt a sense of relief.

"Kane!" I spoke, standing up as he reached me

"Where have you been!?" He asked, placing a hand on my shoulder and inspecting the cut on my cheek. "We all thought you were dead."

"Dead?" I questioned, "How long have I been gone?"

"It's been two days, Mill; you were just gone. We searched the whole town, but you just disappeared."

I looked down at him, flinching as he placed a bandaid on my cheeks, unable to believe I had been gone for that long. I didn't feel hungry, maybe a little thirsty, but I felt as if I was gone for only a few hours.

"What had happened?" Kane asked

"I heard music and followed it. . . Then," the past events felt like a dream. Was any of it real, or did I have some weird fever dream when I ended up in the woods?

"Music?" Kane questioned, furrowing his brows. "You should have gotten me."

"I know," I told him, unsure what else to say. I should have done a lot of things differently.

"Well, let's get you home. Your knees are torn to shreds, and we need to clean them up and get them patched up."

I nodded, looking down at my bleeding knees as my eyes grew wide. "Oh no, Marshmellow!"

"Don't worry, I've ensured she's been fed."

I sighed. "You're the best," I told Kane.

"I know," he replied. "Now come on, your cars at your place. We had it towed, but mine's here."

"You guys sure work fast," I mumbled as I followed him around the house. The acid puddle was still there. The only thing left of Margie was some patches of hair.

I turn to look away, following Kane to his beat-up little car. Getting into the passenger seat, I let my body relax, not having realized how sore my legs truly were.

"You okay?" Kane asked

"Yeah, just exhausted."

"You look pretty beat up," he commented, pulling his car out and getting onto the road.

"What were you doing back at this house in the first place?" I asked Kane

"Since you had disappeared, I kept checking around the house to ensure you hadn't returned."

"Oh, thank you," I told him.

"You're my partner, we have to watch out for each other," he replied, smiling.

"you're a good partner," I told him.

Kane smiled larger at that comment as he focused on the road, so I turned to look out the window.

I don't know what I have seen. It all felt so real, but I am grateful to be alive.

Reaching a hand up, I run a finger over the bandaid across my cheek, thankful to have such a good partner on my side. The scenery rushing past the window lulled me into sleep. My head pressed against the glass of the window,

7

After we returned to my place, the first thing I did was head to the shower. Marshmallow followed me around the whole time, meowing. I suppose she had missed me. Kane cared for her while I showered.

After the shower I stand shirtless in front of the mirror. I still couldn't believe I was gone for two whole days. How could I have gone through two nights and not even notice it, much less grow hungry? I grip the corners of the sink, taking deep breaths to calm my heart, then turn the sink faucet on, splashing my face with cold water.

"Mill," a slight knock on the bathroom door

"Yeah, Kane?" I asked, turning off the water

"The doctors here," he informed me

"Like right at my front door here?"

"Yeah, he's in the kitchen waiting."

I bit my lip, turning to the mirror. My tired emerald eyes looked back at me.

"I'll be out in a few minutes."

"Okay, I'll let him know." Kane's footsteps disappeared from the door as I turned the water back on, splashing my face a few more times to try and wake up.

Simon is a pretty damn good doctor he just sort of creeps me out a little. He's built like a fucking twig with dead blue eyes, well, eye. His left eye is a fake, painted black like he's some goddamn demon. His old-styled Victorian black double-breasted jacket with a tailcoat. His words exactly, he was very clear on his coat and ensured I called it as such.

I grabbed a towel that hung on the sink and dried off my face. I suppose I will see Simon either way. He's in my kitchen. I could go out the back door, but I could smell coffee coming through the door. Kane had made a fresh pot.

Damn him; I mean, I appreciate it, but knowing there's fresh coffee waiting for me, I have to get a cup.

I grab my blue shirt that hung on the door, pulling it over my still-wet hair as it fell loosely over my body.

I wasn't always one for baggy clothing, but my muscles ached along my back to my shoulders, and I didn't feel up to anything tight.

I let myself take a few deep breaths before opening the door. Marshmallow lets out a long, squeaky meow before barreling toward me and running right into my leg.

"Easy there, girl," I tell her with a laugh, scooping her into my arms; she nuzzles against my neck, purring so loud she could be mistaken for a lawn mower.

Carrying her into the kitchen I stop just at the doorway when I notice Simon sitting at the table, his long, slender fingers holding a cup full of steaming coffee, his fancy double chested whatever coat still looking pristine as always, his blue eye putting a chill along my spine while his pure black fake one sits in his left socket. I know he's just a regular guy, his hair graying slicked back with some sort of hair gel, but he always creeped me out, even as a kid; his cold hands always made me shiver when we did checkups.

"Ah, Mill, it's been a long while," Simon spoke clearly and slowly as if choosing his every word carefully.

"Yeah... I've been pretty healthy," I replied, setting Marshmellow on the floor. I took a seat across from him.

"At least until now?" he questioned, raising an eyebrow

"Well, I scraped my knees pretty bad on some rocks."

"Your knees will be fine, Mill. I understand you were lost for two whole days in the woods. I can't imagine you are feeling too well."

"I actually feel pretty good," I admitted. "It only felt like I was in there for maybe twenty minutes? An hour at most."

"You didn't notice any change from day to night?" Simon asked me

"I didn't," I told him, looking down when Kane placed a cup of coffee before me, but Simon started to speak again before I could thank him.

"Did you see anything strange?"

Images flashed in my mind: that deer I had to shoot, then that strange entity from the water. If I told the doctor about them, would that just prove how crazy I had become? My mouth suddenly felt dry, so I took a drink of coffee. Simon's blue eye bore into me.

"No," I lied, unable to bring myself to tell the truth. There were just a lot of trees and confusion. It was hard to find my way around."

"What about the music?" Kane asked, refilling my cup from the pot.

"Oh, right," I replied. It had slipped my mind after coming home

"Music?" Simon asked

"Yeah, I heard it at Margy's. I believe it was from a bagpipe, and it just drew me into the woods," I admitted.

"Interesting," Simon spoke, leaning back into his chair

"What is it?' I asked him

"Your dad had said something rather similar before he passed."

"What?" I asked, dumbfounded.

"He was actually here at home when he heard it. He told me he was worried he was developing some mental illness because your mother couldn't hear the music. It had done the same thing as you, pulling your father to the woods. If it wasn't for your mother, he might have been lost in the woods forever."

"They. . never told me that."

"They might not have wanted to worry you."

"But what does this mean?" I asked him

"It might mean that whatever your father heard might have been more real than he thought."

"I doubt it's anything," I told him, doubting myself as I spoke

"Are you sure you didn't see anything?" Simon asked again, standing this time

"Yes, nothing but woods," I huffed out, annoyed with him already. I just wanted to be left alone; I haven't had time to compose myself besides a short shower.

Simon watched me for a few moments before turning away. "You haven't changed much, have you"

"What do you mean by that?" I asked, narrowing my eyes

"The house, your parents' things are still all up. Shouldn't it be time for you to officially move in, or are you leaving for the big city again?"

"I've been busy."

"How long has it been?"

"It's only been a few months," I told him

"It's been almost a year, boy," he spoke. "It's not good for your health."

"Leave him be," Kane said. "It hasn't even been a year. Give him some time."

I was thankful for Kane's help, but I knew it would only make things worse. Simon's cold eye settled on Kane but shifted back to me.

"I'm just saying that if you keep moping around in a house full of your parents' things, it's not going to help you heal."

"I'll consider it," I told him but only said it to make him stop; Simon is just like a lot of the other older residents of this town, always poking into our lives. I know he's a doctor, but telling me how to live in my house isn't any of his business.

Simon didn't seem pleased with my answer, probably looking past my lie, but stopped bringing it up.

"Get a good meal in you and take today to rest," he told me

What about my knees?" I asked him

"They'll be fine. Just keep them clean," Simon told me as he walked out of the kitchen, so I followed him.

"that's it?" I questioned

"Well, there isn't much else I can do. Just come back to me if you hear anything else, okay? My door is always open," he replied, opening the door and walking out.

I step to the door, watching him make his way to his black hearse without looking back.

"I thought he would at least look at your knees," Kane commented from behind me.

"He's always been weird," I huffed, shutting the door and walking back to the kitchen to pour myself another cup of coffee.

"Mill," Kane spoke softly, walking into the kitchen after me, Marshmallow in his arms.

"Hmm?" I asked, meeting his eyes as I sipped the cup of coffee

"I don't know how to tell you this, but tomorrow is Margy's funeral."

"Tomorrow?" I asked

Kane nodded. "James had gotten a hold of me when you weren't answering any of his calls. He was pretty worried when I told him what had happened, but anyways, it's happening tomorrow,"

"I'm going to have to find my suit," I told him, scratching the back of my neck. "Damn, it's been ages since I've pulled it out."

"Are you going to be okay?" Kane asked, concerned.

I poured another cup of coffee. "Yeah, I can't miss this funeral. I need to be there for James."

"I'll be there too," Kane informed me. "So if you don't feel well, I got your back."

"Thanks, Kane," I told him. "What time is the funeral?" I asked him

"It's pretty early," he informed me. "So we might want to get to bed soon; I hope you're okay with me staying over."

"What time is it?" I questioned, looking at the clock on the stove. It was about six.

"you've been through a lot, Mill. I don't think the Boss would mind if you rest; besides, by the time we even get to the station, it'll be dark."

I sighed and sat my mug down. "Fine, I'll sleep," I told him. I was feeling pretty fatigued anyway.

"Do you want to eat anything before bed?" Kane asked as he moved to the fridge

"I'll just do a muffin," I replied, opening the cabinet. I was thankful I still had one left, so I pulled it from the container and took a bite.

"You're having a real breakfast then," Kane informed me

"If you're cooking, I'll eat it," I told him, making my way to the doorway. "There should be blankets and a pillow in the living room already, so you're welcome to sleep on the couch."

"Thanks, Mill, I'll see you in the morning."

I nod and walk to my room, shutting the door. The silence surrounds me like a blanket.

I took another bite from the muffin and put the reminder on the dresser. I can hear Kane playing with Marshmallow outside the room, thankful he can keep her busy. I don't think I have the energy for her.

I turn to the closet, walking over. I open it and find the old, worn suit my father used to wear. I am relieved to know it is still in there. I finally let myself crawl into the bed, my head hitting the soft pillow like a brick.

Damn, I've never been this tired my entire life, but besides that small nap in the car, I suppose I hadn't slept for two whole days.

Such a strange thing to happen. I still don't understand what happened to me, but I guess I can just be thankful I'm still alive.

Pulling the blanket over my shoulders, it didn't take me long to fall into a heavy sleep, my aching muscles finally relaxing.

8

The next day, I woke up to a knock at my bedroom door, which caused me to groan. I sat up feeling pretty groggy still. Turning to the window, I noticed that it was still pretty dark outside.

"Can I come in?" Kane asked through the door.

"Sure," I croaked out.

Kane opened the door, light seeping in from the crack as Marshmellow bolted in immediately, jumping on the bed and curling up beside me.

"How are you feeling?" Kane asked, stepping further into the room with a red mug in his hand

"I think I feel alright," I told him. "Maybe a little nauseous."

"You might just be hungry," he commented, stepping further in as he handed me the mug. There's a breakfast setup; we should prepare for the funeral."

"What time is it?" I asked him, taking the mug. The hot cup felt incredible against my hands.

"It's 4 a.m. currently. The funeral will start at about seven, giving us time to prepare."

"you said you made breakfast?" I asked

"Yeah, it's still warm, so you might want to get some now."

"Okay, I'll be there in just a minute."

"Take your time," Kane told me, leaving my room and closing the door behind him.

I look down at my mug, drinking the blissful coffee, Marshmellow purring against my leg, so I lean forward to scratch her chin.

"Such a good girl," I told her, finishing my coffee and getting out of bed.

I leave the bedroom, figuring I'll get breakfast before I change into the suit. There is no way I will risk dropping something on it. I hear the shower turn on from the bathroom. Kane must be using it. He sure made himself cozy, though. I suppose it's not so bad; it helps make this house seem less empty.

Marshmellow brushed against my leg and then suddenly jolted into the kitchen, so I followed her where she tackled her food bowl, flipping it around.

"You don't need to be so dramatic," I told her, picking the bowl up and noticing the large setup on the table.

Kane had prepared pancakes and bacon with several different syrups and a small amount of butter. Did I own any of this?

Marshmellow lets out a loud meow, startling me.

"Okay, Your Highness, I'm getting your food," I told her, opening the top drawer and finding her cat food. Kane must have put it in here from the car. Damn, I need to buy him a thank-you gift or something.

Taking one of the cans of cat food, I pry it open, dumping the wet food into a bowl before placing it down for Marshmellow, who greedily ate like she'd never had food before.

"I'm pretty sure Kane fed you, but I suppose this is how you always ate," I said, shaking my head. I moved to sit at the table, a little overwhelmed by the amount of food Kane had prepared.

He must have gotten up pretty early to make all of this.

Looking over it all, I grab a few pancakes, butter them, and then use one of the sugary syrups before placing some bacon onto my plate and quickly eating it. Man, I was hungry. The food on my plate did not last long, leaving me feeling bloated but good. I hadn't had a meal like that in a long while.

I turn to see Marshmellow's empty food dish and she's nowhere to be seen. But hearing the bathroom door open, I'm pretty sure she's begging Kane for food now.

Getting up, I look around the counter. Where the hell did I put that mug? Did I leave it in my room? Not wanting to walk back, I grab my thermos sitting by the pot and pour coffee into it.

"You got some food?" Kane asked as he walked into the kitchen, his hair still damp.

"Yeah, it was fantastic," I told him, sipping my coffee.

"I'm glad to hear," Kane said, sitting at the table. Marshmellow padded in, finding a cozy spot on one of the chairs.

"I'm going to get ready," I told Kane

"Alright, I'll be here," he replied, filling a plate.

I gave a nod and walked to my bedroom, shutting the door. The red mug I had misplaced sat right on my nightstand, but for now, I ignored it. I walked to the closet where the suit was located, pulling it out fully.

It's a little worn, but it still looks pretty good. A plain black suit, just as plain as you can expect, I guess. My father was always good at taking care of his clothing, so after this, maybe I'll get it stored away so it doesn't get ruined. Along with my mom's clothing, she still had some pretty lovely dresses I didn't know what to do with.

Whenever I consider packing their things up or moving something, it gives me this sense of panic. I just couldn't bring myself to change anything around here yet like; once I do, they're officially gone. If I keep it the same, it still feels like they are around.

Biting my lip, I stripped to my boxers and slipped on the suit. The shoulders were a little tight, but it wasn't too bad; it was manageable for at least a day.

I just need a tie now, so I walk to my dresser and dig around in the underwear drawer, finding a white tie. I pull it out and clumsily tie it on. I forgot how long it's been since I wore a tie. Hopefully, James doesn't mind that it's a little crooked.

Staring at myself in the mirror, I hear Kane call for me

"We should get going!"

"Coming!" I called back, staring at myself for a few more moments before I pried my eyes away and left the room. I found Kane at the front door in a black suit with a bright pink tie neatly around his neck.

I walk over, and grab my fedora from its hook, then slip on my shoes

"Are you sure you want to wear that?" Kane asked, gesturing to my hat

"I don't think you can judge me with that blinding tie," I joked

"I like color," he told me

"Nothing wrong with it. You have your pink tie, and I have my fedora."

"Alright, I suppose you always wear it anyway," he said

"It's my signature," I joked, grabbing my overcoat and slipping it over my suit. I checked the pockets for my phone and other items inside. Feeling them there, I reached for the hook by the door where my gun and holster hung.

"Do we need to bring our guns?" Kane asked

"I like to keep it on me; you never know what might happen," I informed him, slipping the holster onto my waist, hidden by my coat.

"Mines in the car," he told me, opening the front door

"Might not be the best place for it," I informed him, following him out. "Be good, Marshmellow!" I shouted before shutting the door.

"I forgot about it. I was worried about you," Kane told me.

"I can let it slide," I told him, walking to my car

"You sure you can drive?" Kane asked

"I'll be okay," I replied, getting inside, and he hesitantly got into the passenger seat.

"Alright, let's get going," I said, suddenly anxious about this. I always hated funerals. My parents were the worst; maybe I'm just worried about James. His dad passed away years ago, and now he had lost his mother. It's not easy, and I just hope I can be there for him.

Trying to keep focus, I drove onto the main road toward the town

"Oh, shit, where even is the funeral?" I asked Kane

"It's at the cemetery," Kane responded

"I haven't been over there in a long while," I told him

There isn't much reason to go all the way out there typically."

"I suppose unless you're visiting loved ones or attending church, but I don't think This town has many religious people."

"Victor is at the church pretty often, I believe, and I know Debbie and a few other residents here go every Sunday, but they are the only ones I know who do."

"I'm not personally religious, but even if I was, it's too much of a hassle driving out there."

"It's worth it if you actually enjoy it. I remember my folks dragging me all the way over there in the early morning. It was always so cold and boring."

"I'm glad my parents weren't religious," I said, smiling. "I only went there as a kid to help set up events. Victor always paid us kids, so James and I always showed up to set chairs or help manage food."

"I bet Victor hoped it would get you guys to join the church," Kane joked

"I'm sure it was, but he was always respectful, never forced us, and I'm sure he just enjoyed the help even if he was paying for it."

"Victor always creeped me out," Kane admitted

"He's just a serious guy," I told him.

As we make it into the town, I take a right onto the road where the neighborhood houses are, following the trail back towards the trees to a small dirt road.

"It's pretty ballsy of them to put the church so deep into the woods," I mention, my car shaking against the rough terrain.

"Maybe they thought it gave the church personality," Kane joked as we reached a large clearing.

The old white church sat far off along the edge of the forest. It stood taller than the trees, with a big bell at the top and big stained-glass windows along the sides of it. One big stained-glass window up high in the tower led to the bell.

The parking lot is just a tiny gravel spot with logs to separate the spaces. Most of the spots were already filled, so I parked off to the far right along the trees' edge to leave the room.

The cemetery took up the rest of the ample space beside the church. A worn white fence surrounded the few acres of land. A hump formed about halfway, making it hard to see the rest of the commentary, and since I couldn't see anyone, I suppose they were on the other side of that small hill.

"How are you feeling?" Kane asked

"Exhausted, but I'll be okay," I told him, getting out of the car.

Feeling something suddenly wet, I wiped my cheek, feeling a slight sting. I had forgotten I got a cut there. Looking up, I could see storm clouds forming.

"Shit, it's going to rain," I said

"I don't have an umbrella," Kane told me

"I got one in the trunk," I replied, walking around, pushing the button, and letting the trunk shoot open. My red umbrella was sitting exactly where I expected it to be. I pulled it out and handed it to Kane.

"You don't want to hold it?" Kane asked, opening the umbrella up

"we can just share it," I told him, shutting the trunk.

"I guess we just walk to the church and hope we see them?" Kane asked, looking around

"I suppose with the weather starting to turn, I can't imagine they would be outside," I told him, walking towards the church.

Kane kept the umbrella over us as it started to rain a little more; the droplets' patter sounded loud against the umbrella's top, and the wind began to pick up.

When we reached the church's door, I paused before we could go inside, noticing a small group of people at the forest edge beside the fence. I guess they were burying her pretty close to the forest.

"We should head over there," I told Kane. Already walking, Kane jogged up beside me.

"why are they putting her so far away?"

"Maybe they are running out of room," I told him, looking down, careful to keep on the small path. I did not want to step on a gravestone or over a body.

As we reached the small group, Victor was wearing his pastor's clothing, standing in front of the group with a Bible in hand, talking about whatever gospel which I zoned out, and focused on the group.

James stood close to Victor, holding a pink umbrella with black stripes. When our eyes met, he gave me a soft smile, nodding his head to gesture Kane and me to join in. So I stepped over to stand beside Gary, who wore a black suit and held a dark wood cane in his right hand.

Scarlet stood in a beautiful dark blue dress to his left, holding an umbrella up for Gary and herself. Bob wore his work uniform with a black overcoat to our right, but I couldn't see his brother Mike anywhere. The only other person here was Luke, who stood by Bob. Our eyes met for only a moment, and I looked away when I heard Victor finish the gospel speaking.

Victor started on some speech about everlasting life and about

Margy's spirit; I always struggled to focus entirely on these sorts of speeches, my eyes wandering down to the casket in between us, a beautiful red oak. I believe the hole had already been dug, the soft dirt turning dark as the rain dropped on it.

I focus back on Victor, who spoke about Margy's life.

Damn, I can't focus on it. All I can focus on is the rain hitting the umbrella and how devastated James looks.

Losing a parent is rough, but finding your parent dead must be rough. Margy wasn't in good shape when I saw her. I couldn't imagine what James felt when he found her.

"I need a few volunteers to help lower Margy," Victor suddenly spoke, pulling me back into the present. I was ready to volunteer, but Kane handed me the umbrella and stepped forward while Bob, Luke, and Scarlet took the other spots.

I suppose it was for the best. I was more than ready to help, but my muscles still ached a little as the four helped lower Margy into the hole using ropes to get her safely down. Then Bob took a shovel to put dirt over her from the pile near us. Kane came back to my side to stand under the umbrella.

I watched Bob for a few moments when James walked over to stand beside me

"Thanks for coming," he told me

"I wouldn't have missed it for anything," I told him.

"I heard what happened. Was it scary being lost in those woods?" James asked. His voice cracked a little, and his eyes watered. It wasn't hard to see that he was trying not to cry.

"Honestly, I didn't even realize two days had passed. It was like one long day."

"That's so weird," he commented, staring forward at the hole Bob was filling, Luke helping him.

"What are you going to do now?" I asked James

"I'm going to take a break from work and do what I should have done years ago."

"What's that?" I asked, turning to him

"I'm going to clean up Mom's place. I'll probably leave her fairy homes, but I'll also take care of her cats and fix up the old place."

"Well, if you ever need help, just give me a ring, okay?" I offered.

"Thanks, but for now, I'm going through boxes and deciding what I want to keep."

"I have not even done that yet," I admitted

"It'll probably take me a while, too. I honestly want to get the cats under control. I can't keep all of them, but I plan to keep her favorites and adopt the others out."

"I'm glad you'll get that under control. It's gotten a little crazy lately."

"I feel bad, but they need to be fixed and checked for worms. I'm having animal control come in from a neighboring town to help."

"I hope that works out for you," I told him, placing a hand on his shoulder to give a sense of comfort. I know he was trying hard to keep it together.

"Mill," I suddenly heard my name called, so I turned around to see Scarlet.

"Hey, Scarlet," I spoke.

"How are you feeling?" she asked

"I feel more or less like myself," I told her

Scarlet nodded, almost hesitating for a moment. "Could I speak to you and Kane for a moment?"

"uh, sure?" I told her, glancing at James, who offered a smile, stepping over to talk with Gary.

"If this is work-related..." I started Scarlet cutting me off

"We got a tip on who killed Nora," She whispered

"You did?" I asked shocked

"Who?!" Kane asked

"Coby," Scarlet answered

"Coby?" I questioned

"We got a call from Declan claiming he saw something suspicious from Coby that day."

"Have you done anything about it yet?" I asked

"We got the call only this morning, and Benny tried to talk with him, but Coby won't budge. Do you think you can try?"

"The call isn't good enough to arrest him?" Kane asked

"We can't find evidence that he's guilty," Scarlet told him.

"What do you want us to do?" I asked her

"You are the best at getting people to talk. I know this isn't the greatest timing, but speaking with Coby now might be a good element of surprise."

I sighed, looking over at James, who was now talking with Victor and Luke. "Fine.," I told her hesitantly,

I didn't want to leave James during his time of need, but knowing him well enough, he would probably tell me to go and find the person who had done this.

"Are you sure?" Kane asked

"Scarlet's right. He would expect us to be here, so showing up might throw him off his game," I told him.

"Thank you, Mill. If you can find proof, we can stop any more of this pain and finally settle those who died."

"I'll. . . We'll try our best," I told her. "let James know I'm working on the case."

"You don't want to talk to him?" Scarlet asked

I shook my head, not giving her an answer. I turned back to the car, Kane beside me, the umbrella still in my left hand, keeping us dry.

"You okay?" Kane asked

"I will be; my mind has just been a little overwhelmed lately."

"I'm not surprised. Will you be able to speak with Coby?"

"Once we get there I'll go into auto mode. It'll be easy," I told Kane.

the two of us get to my car and I felt Kane grip my left arm, stopping me

"Mill, are you sure? We're leaving a funeral for work, and you haven't even been able to settle down since returning."

I pull my arm away, dropping the umbrella. "I said I would be fine, now either get in the car or I'm leaving you here," I snapped.

Kane sighed, picking up the umbrella. "I'm sorry, I just. . ."

"No, I'm sorry. You're right. It's been a lot, but this might be our best chance. I promise I'll take a break when we are done, okay?"

This seemed to satisfy Kane for now as he closed the umbrella

"I'm holding you to it," he spoke before getting into the car, and I followed suit.

I started my car and backed out from the spot, heading out onto the bumpy road again as we headed back into Northwood. The drive to the mechanic shop wasn't far from the neighborhood as I drove past the houses and took a right; between the inn and the grocery store is where the mechanic shop sits.

Seeing it, I took the right into the parking space. It had double garage doors, but both were currently closed and a small office was to the left, so I parked in front of it and shut the car off.

"What do we say?" Kane asked

"Let me do the talking," I told him. "he may be a little touchy seeing us, so we need to be careful what we say."

"I'll just observe."

"Observe and stay beside me," I tell him, getting out of the car.

This was the sort of thing I would do in the big city. Still, to people I didn't know, having to speak to Coby as a potential murderer felt... uneasy, like I was a child talking to an adult.

Swallowing my nerves, I push open the door to the office, the state of it alarming.

The metal shelves that lined the wall were open and papers were scattered about. Pictures of old cars from the wall shattered on the floor, along with documents from the shelves on the floor. The desk at the end of the room was a cluttered mess, with the laptop smashed against it.

Coby sat hunched in the chair with his right hand on the desk, his dark blue overalls stained in blood. His bald head had a large gash in it as if he ran his head into a wall.

A large knife was on the floor by the desk, and a gash was taken out of his right arm like he had carved a piece of his flesh out. The carved flesh just lying on the desk was bloodied.

"Coby?" I asked, shocked by the sight. Time suddenly moved slowly. I'd seen horrific sights before, but to see Coby in this scene was completely surprising.

Coby's head lulled around, his blue eyes meeting mine, his right eye red as if irritated.

"I didn't do it!" He screamed out suddenly, thrashing around against the desk.

Kane took my left arm, tugging me slightly to pull me out, but I stayed firm.

"Coby, please calm down!" I begged him. The sight of him made my stomach twist.

"Mill, we need to call Scarlet," Kane hissed.

Kane was right. Whatever was happening here, there wasn't anything we could do. We needed backup. Coby is too big of a guy for Kane and me to restrain in a state like this.

"They did it! They control everything!" Coby spat out, his uninjured hand reaching for a drawer on the desk and pulling something out that glinted in the light.

"Coby, no!" I shouted, but it was too late, the shock of the impact hitting my right shoulder before I could even shift.

"Mill!" I could hear Kane, but it sounded distant.

I stumbled back in shock from being shot in the shoulder, the pain not yet settling in as I felt Kane pull something from my waist, my left hand pressing against my shoulder as I tried to stop the bleeding when another ear-piercing noise wracked my head.

I turn to Kane, who held my gun. Coby's lifeless body slumped over his desk, blood splattered across the wall behind him; Kane had gotten him right in the head.

"Mill, stay with me," Kane's voice suddenly softened as I slumped back into the wall. I was losing a lot of blood, and I couldn't bring myself out of shock. Time stopped being slow and began moving far too fast, my vision blurring and Kane talking nonstop, gently slapping my cheek, trying to keep me awake, but it wasn't working.

I couldn't keep my eyes open as they grew too heavy and I passed out.

9

When I open my eyes, a coldness wraps around my body in a vice grip, numbing my fingers and toes and forcing me to shiver.

"What happened?" I asked myself, my voice echoing around me.

Sitting up, I squinted my eyes, but the world around me was so dark I couldn't see a damn thing, the rough ground hurting my ass as I shifted. Rubbing my palms over the ground to try and get a sense of where I was, but all it did was remind me of the lake when I used to swim. The slick mossy rocks that would cover the bed and threaten to slip you, my left palm brushing over a small pool of water. Was I in the woods again?

The air smelled fishy and moist as if I were in a cave beside some water, but I don't recall knowing any caves.

Could this be a dream? I pinch my right arm, flinching from the pain. I was indeed awake, but how did I end up here? What happened?

Something happened. . . Right when I was at Margy's funeral, James looked so sad. Did I comfort him?

"Damnit," I growled, frustrated. I brought my left hand up to my temples, trying to remember, but my memory was fuzzy.

I move to my knees and push myself up to stand, my legs shaking beneath my weight, causing me to fall again, struggling to find my strength.

Did I die? How would I have died? I was doing something... That's right, I was shot! My left hand instinctively reached my right shoulder, but everything was fine, at least pain-wise. The numbing cold made it hard to feel anything, but I was able to move my right arm as if it had healed?

Or maybe I was dead, having bled out on the floor before anyone could help me... That was a scary thought, poor Kane, he must be scared all alone.

"You should be concerned for yourself," a cacophony of voices rang, causing my ears to ache.

"Where am I?" I asked, turning my head, but all I could see was darkness

"You are in the abyss, where you belong," the voices spoke. It was like hundreds of voices of all ages, women and men, speaking simultaneously. I've heard something like this before... Yeah, back in the woods, the thing in the water that screamed.

"What do you mean where I belong?" I asked the creature, trying to seek it out in the darkness, but it was hopeless

"You don't know much, do you" the thing spoke, pushing my ears to their limits.

"Am I dead?"

It was silent for a long time before finally speaking, "No, you'll never truly die. Your soul has been marked. I own you."

I furrowed my brows, even more confused. "Can you be more clear?" I asked, trying to understand what was happening.

There was another long silence when something stirred in front of me as a pulse of dark blue light shot out, illuminating the circular space I stood in for only a moment until another pulse shot out the walls cracking, illuminating a blue, reminding me of a frozen lake as the pulsing light traveled across the ground, the mossy rocks illuminated by the blue light.

I could see the walls swirling like water. The creature only a few feet from me looked all too familiar, with glowing red eyes and a body made of water.

"Are you scared?" it's voices echoed.

"No," I told it, narrowing my eyes, terrified, but I couldn't show it fear. "I want answers."

A low singular voice trembled from the creature like laughter. "You're a brave soul," the single voice spoke before the cacophony of the others joined in again. "I'll allow your questions."

I stood up finally, my legs still shaky, but I managed to keep myself upright this time.

"First, I want to know where I am," I spoke. I didn't want to believe any of this was real, but I had to have answers if it was.

"I already told you."

"Right, the abyss," I spoke, repeating its words from before, "but I don't know where that is."

"It's the line between the water spirits and the living world, my domain."

"Water spirits?" I asked, bringing my left hand to my temple to rub it. "This has to be some fever dream."

A sudden strike of pain wracked against my right shoulder, forcing me to a knee.

"Does that feel fake?" the creature asked

I grit my teeth and look at my bleeding shoulder. "What did you do?"

"I merely allowed you to feel the pain of your injury. You're currently lying in a hospital bed on the verge of death; I'm here to claim you. Is that enough to satisfy your wonder?"

"No!" I snarled, "Tell me, how did I become marked, and can I stop it?"

the beast let out a long, exhausted breath. "you're a threat to their plans. They want you gone for good, so they gave you to me."

"Who are they," I asked through gritted teeth. I had to know the answers

"I'm unable to answer that. As for stopping this, we have to make a deal."

"a deal?" I questioned, looking at it

"Yes, a deal."

"What do you want?" I asked, knowing this wouldn't end well for me.

"I want your soul."

I gulped. "Is there anything else you would want?"

"The only way out would be to sacrifice someone for me."

"so, trade my soul for another?" I asked

"You catch on fast," it spoke, the deeper voice seeming amused while the other mixed voices seemed hesitant and fearful.

I took a heavy breath. I couldn't doom someone else to a fate like this.

"Can you give me more time?" I asked it

the creature seemed amused by this as its red eyes bore into mine. "Yes," it spoke

"Really?" I asked, surprised it had agreed so soon.

The creature's laughter filled the room, the cacophony of voices causing me to get a headache. It moved across the room swiftly to tower over me, a chill grasping my body.

"It's going to be fun watching you struggle."

I tried to speak, but I suddenly couldn't find my voice. The creature let out a sickening laughter. A sudden wave of warmth spread across my body, blurring my vision and shifting the world around me until everything went dark.

"Hey, he's coming back," a woman spoke to my right

"He's finally stable," said a man to my left.

Things were moving so quickly that my lungs ached as I took in a deep breath, my heart thumping in my chest as a machine to my left beeped along with it.

I open my eyes slowly only to be blinded by a light, so I shut them again.

"Mill, can you hear me?" the woman asked

"Yeah," I forced out, my throat sore and dry.

"Do you remember what happened?" She asked

I opened my right eye to look at the woman, her blond hair cut short into a pixy cut, her green eyes almost glowing against all the light in the room.

"I was shot..." I told her

She nodded. "You were, but you are safe now; you should make a full recovery."

"Where Kane?" I asked

"He's in the waiting room. Once you feel better, we'll let you have visitors."

I nodded, opening my left eye and letting it adjust to the room's bright lighting, glancing at the man to my left side cleaning up supplies. His black hair was longer and tied back into a bun. I could only see his back, a pair of blue scrubs covering his body, while the lady wore the same scrubs but with a white doctor's coat over them.

"Could I have some water?" I asked, turning back to face her

"I'll have Gene here get you a menu for our kitchen. Get some water and something easy to eat," she told me

"I'll take a look over it," I told her

"I'll go get that now," Gene said, turning around so I could see his brown eyes. I'll be right back," he added, disappearing out the door to the room's left. Finally, I started taking in my surroundings now that I'd come out of my dazed state.

It wasn't much. There was a door on the left and a small window on the right. My bed was alone against the back wall, right in the middle, with a TV hanging up on the wall. A rather comfortable-looking armchair close to the window.

"Are you okay?" the woman asked

"yeah, I think I'm still just in shock."

"you went through something pretty traumatic. You are still on some heavy pain meds, but your shoulder will be pretty sore for a while."

I nodded, letting myself fully relax, looking down at my body. An IV was attached to my left wrist with some clear liquid dripping through the pipe while my left shoulder was bandaged up, a thin pink blanket over me, but I could see my chest, and I was in a blue hospital gown.

"Where is my stuff?" I asked her

"Kane has your belongings, though your suit is ruined. We had to cut it off, sorry,"

"Damn," I spoke, closing my eyes. That was my father's suit. I can't believe it's destroyed. I doubt I could get it fixed.

"I can see if Kane has any spare clothing for you. If anything, we have a gift shop that might have some clothing," she reassured me.

"Thanks. I'm sure I'll get it figured out." I told her I didn't want to talk about how that suit was my dad's; it couldn't be fixed now, and I didn't want sympathy.

"What's your name?" I asked her

"Oh, sorry. It's Jasmine," she told me, offering me a kind smile. I'll be your primary doctor while you are here. We will monitor you for the night, and if all looks good, we'll release you in the morning."

"I need to get home to my cat," I told her, worried about Marshmellow

"Get some food in you before we start discussing letting you out early. You were shot yesterday, Mill. Let's not rush this."

I sighed. "Okay, I'll eat something," I told her, knowing the faster I cooperate, the quicker the process.

"Good, you hang tight here. Gene should be back soon with a menu. If you need anything, he'll be the one to ask," Jasmine told me.

"Thank you," I told her, watching as she moved around to the door, leaving me alone with the beeping machine.

I turned to the right to look out the window, which only gave me a view of the parking lot. A few random cars parked around with woods off in the distance.

Mora is a small town about an hour or so from Northwood. It has the closest hospital, so it's no surprise I ended up here; it has been a long while since I've been here.

A slight knock on the door startles me a little as I look over to see Gene walk in.

"Sorry that took too long," he apologized, striding over and handing me a small menu.

I take the menu in my left hand, glancing over it. The options were pretty limited.

"Anything looking good? I can get your order in right away," he told me

"Uh, I'll do the mashed potatoes and a coffee?" I told him

"Alright," he said, taking the menu. "I'll get that to the kitchen. If you need anything, just let us know," he said, leaving me alone again.

I look up at the stand beside me that contains the fluids for my IV. I have always hated those things, especially the ones attached to my left wrist. At least I was asleep for the process, I suppose.

I lay my head against the thin pillow, wishing I was home. The smell of cleaners filled the air, making me feel nauseous. Someone knocked on the door and opened it.

It was Gene again. He had a platter, which he placed on a small table beside the IV.

"This is your food. Take your time. I'll let Jasmine know you got it, and we'll send in your friend here in a bit," he explained.

"Thanks," I told him as he left once again. The silence in the room started to get to me, but I couldn't find the remote for the small TV, so I gave up and pressed the button to make the bed lift, so I was sitting up.

Pulling the table closer with my left arm, keeping my right one to my side, I pull the lid off to a sad bowl of mashed potatoes and an old-smelling coffee, little creamer cups, and butter squares beside them.

I put the bowl of mashed potatoes on my lap and just ate it straight. It was one of those pre-packet ones, I'm pretty sure, but it wasn't bad; the coffee tasted burnt, so I dumped a few cups of the creamer crap into it to help. There was yet another knock on the door before it opened, Kane walking in with a bag in his hand.

"Kane!" I said, thankful to see a familiar face

"Hey, how are you feeling?" he asked

"I'm a little too drugged up to know for sure."

"Oh yeah, I bet you'll be sore once we get out of here."

"How are things back home?" I asked

"I've been here with you since yesterday, but Scarlet has kept me updated on what's happening."

"Anything I should know?" I asked him

"Maybe we should wait until. ."

"It's okay, please. I need to know," I asked him.

Kane hesitated, but ultimately nodded. "Well, Coby didn't make it. I had shot him in the leg after he shot you, but he had lost so much already, cutting out that chunk of his flesh."

"Did you find out why he had done that?" I asked him

"I spoke to Poppy over the phone, and she told me he had carved out a tattoo."

"A tattoo?" I asked

"Yeah, it was a symbol she's never seen before, so she's been looking into it."

"Weird," I said, looking away to process what he had said, only to look back when he spoke again.

"Debbie and John are missing."

"What do you mean missing?"

"Scarlet and Ryker had done some investigating, and when they went to talk with them, they were just gone."

"Any clues as to where?"

Kane shook his head. "They even searched their homes and found no evidence of where they went or if it's related to the current case, but I can only imagine it's all connected."

"Is that everything?" I asked him

"for now, yeah, the doctor told me she'll be here soon to check you out and see if you can go home."

"Let's hope. I want to get home to Marshmellow," I told him

"Oh right, Luke got a hold of me. I told him what had happened, and he went by your place and fed her."

"Oh good," I said, relieved, "at least she got something."

"she's well taken care of, don't worry," he reassured me

"Thank you, Kane. You sure got things handled, don't you?"

"I'm your partner, of course, I got your back."

"Oh right, what's that bag you have?" I asked him

"It's some clothing for you. I picked up a few things at the gift shop for you to wear back home."

"Oh, that's a relief. I was a little worried I'd have to wear this gown."

"I wouldn't let that happen," Kane chuckled, looking back when there was a knock on the door, and Jasmine came in.

"I was told someone wanted an early checkout?" she asked

"If possible," I told her.

Jasmine nodded and walked over to me, taking the coffee out of my hand, placing it on the table, and rolling it away.

"Take deep breaths," she said softly.

I do as she says as she places a Stethoscope on my chest. The cold metal sends a chill up my spine as she moves it to a few spots before removing it.

"Okay, we are going to have you sit up. Let's get that injured arm into a sling," Jasmine said, placing a white cloth over my head and gently lifting my right arm into the sling. A minor ache washed over my shoulder, but with the pain meds they had me on, I didn't feel too much. My arm felt snug in the cloth.

"We'll send you with some meds, but I can't guarantee it'll be completely pain-free later," she told me.

"That's fine," I told her.

"Alright, now let's get you up," she spoke gently, removing the IV from my arm. The little baggy emptied anyway as she guided me off the bed.

My feet touched the floor, the cold making me shudder, and my legs felt a little wobbly, but overall, I could stand without too much of an issue.

"You don't feel dizzy?" She asked me, keeping a grip on my left arm.

"No, I think I'll be fine," I tell her.

"Alright, well, I can't force you to stay. Change into some clothing, and we'll have you sign something before you leave," she spoke, letting go of my arm. "Just make sure to keep it easy and keep your bandages clean. You'll get a paper for all your care."

"Thank you," I told her as she slowly backed away

"Okay, if you feel anything odd, just let us know," she said before leaving.

"Do you want some help?" Kane stepped forward, placing the bag he had been holding on the bed

"I should be okay on my own," I tell him

"Are you sure?" He asked

I nod. "I will, don't worry, this isn't my first time in a cast."

"Why am I not surprised" Kane chuckled. "right, just call if you need me," he said, stepping out and shutting the door, though I wouldn't doubt that he was waiting right on the other side.

Turning to the bag on the bed, I dump it out to find a pair of tan cargo shorts, blue socks, a shirt with a wolf, and my shoes.

This was definitely not my style, but it was better than walking out of here wearing one of these flimsy gowns, so I got myself changed.

The shirt was oversized on me, which made it easier to pull on. The right sleeve was over my arm since I couldn't put it through the hole, and the cargo pants were a little tight but fit well otherwise.

One last thing was my shoes, so I reached to grab them only to notice something odd on the palm of my left hand, so I turned it to find an unfamiliar drawing.

It looked like an eye? Just a simple one with an oval for the pupil and then a couple of lines for the outline of the eye. I never had this before, so how did I get this? I can't imagine the doctors putting this on me, and Kane didn't seem like the type to pull a joke like this?

I look around the room, seeing the sink in the far corner. I walk over to it, turn it on, and run my hand under the water; the ink does not seem to smear, so I clumsily take a paper towel with one hand. It was definitely awkward, but still, it didn't come off.

A little annoyed, I turned the sink off and stared at the mark on my hand. A thought suddenly crossed my mind: This mark... It came from that water spirit. I don't know how I knew this, but I just knew it was from it.

Was this some sick joke of a mark? Like, it's always watching? Waiting until it can claim me? It would be so easy to deny its existence... But I don't think I mentally could. There's this chill in my bones I don't think I'll ever get rid of.

"Mill?" Kane's voice came through the door and rattled me back to reality

"Yeah?" I asked with a shaky breath,

"Is everything okay?"

"Yeah...Yeah! I'm done. You can come in," I tell him, clenching my hand into a fist. I'll have to deal with this after I solve this murder case before anyone else ends up hurt.

The door opened and Kane stepped inside with Gene beside him

"I have some papers for you to sign, then you are allowed to leave," Gene told me

"Alright," I say, walking over, Gene holding the clipboard with the paper on it, which was just basic medical crap I honestly didn't bother to read. I've been to hospitals before, so I signed it with his pen.

"Thank you. Here is this," Gene said, handing me a set of stapled papers. We'll send a prescription of the pain meds you need to the Northwood shop, so by the time you get into town, they should be ready."

"Thank you," I tell him, taking the paper which Kane took to hold onto for me

Gene nodded and left, leaving the two of us alone.

"Your stuff is in my car. Sorry I couldn't get you any better clothing," Kane apologized.

"It's fine," I tell him, walking to the door. "Let's just get home. . . I'm tired."

Kane only gave me a nod and led me out of the hospital. The layout was ordinary and what you would expect a hospital to be; it was small, too, with only three floors. We were on the second floor, so we took an elevator and navigated the unsettling white halls to the large front doors.

The wind made my hair a mess as a gust hit us suddenly when stepping out of the building.

"it feels like there might be a storm," Kane commented, turning to me. "Stay here; I'll grab the car."

Before I could speak, he was off into the large parking lot, leaving me awkwardly at the front door; my legs were fine. Still, it would be even more awkward if I followed now since he was already in his car, so I just waited. Another gust of wind rushed past me, rustling the branches from small trees lined by the building.

Kane's little car pulled beside me, and I opened the door, dropping into the passenger seat.

"Are you feeling any pain?" Kane asked

"No, not yet, but I'm sure I will soon. We'll have to stop and get the meds at the grocery shop when we get into town."

"That's not a problem; why don't you get some rest for now?" Kane suggested

"It's a pretty long drive, are you sure?"

"Only like an hour, I'll be fine. Get some shut-eye. Your body is going to need as much rest as it can get."

I glanced at him, his green eyes focused on the road as he twisted the knob on his radio, soft music filling the car.

"Okay, wake me up when we're almost there."

"I will," Kane spoke softly.

I breathed heavily, resting my forehead against the chill window, my sleeved shoulder comfortable in my shirt as I watched the last of the buildings turn into trees, the ride lulling me into sleep.

10

I woke feeling groggy, my forehead sore from being pressed against the window. Kane gently shook my left shoulder, so I turned to him, an aching pain flowing in my right shoulder.

"We're at the store. You can stay here. I'll go grab it for you, okay?"

"Oh wait, you need permission," I said, looking around my lap, but I didn't know where any of my items were

"The doctor put me down as someone who could pick it up for you. Don't worry; I just didn't want you to freak out when you woke up and I was gone," he said, smiling as he exited the car. He left me alone with the car running and some pop song playing. I felt like a dog but was thankful I didn't have to get up.

I lift my left hand to stare at the drawing, though I have a feeling it's a permanent tattoo that'll stay with me for the rest of my life, or at least until that thing deems it's time for it to take me. I would like to know if it's something I could escape. My knowledge of such an unknown thing was nothing, but I'm a detective; I'll figure it out. I have to.

A buzzing startled me. I looked around the middle console when I realized it was coming from the jockey box. I popped it open to find my wallet, gun and holster, notepad, and phone.

My phone was lit up and vibrating, so I picked it up, seeing the caller ID was Poppy.

Answering, I didn't get a single word in. Screaming filled the other end, Poppy's screaming.

"Poppy!?" I called out

"Help, oh my god, HEL~" it cuts off. I've never heard such a high-pitched shriek come from her before. The pain in it caused my body to shiver, causing me to freeze momentarily, snapping back into reality only when Kane had returned.

"Mill?" he asked.

I turned to him, my heart in my ears. "We need to get to the station now, no questions," I said urgently, and he must have sensed that because he slid into the car and immediately drove onto the road toward the station.

"What is going on?"

"I got a call from Poppy begging for help," I tell him, dialing my phone, but I couldn't get a hold of Scarlet, Ryker, the Boss, or even Benny. Where the hell was everyone? It just kept going to voice mail for them all.

"I think we're on our own," I tell him, pulling my gun from the jockey box

"What are we even doing? you're still injured!" Kane protested

"I am not going to stand idly by if Poppy is in danger," I told him

Kane sighed but nodded as he parked crookedly in front of the station. The only car was Poppy's blue van

"Good, I guess, right?" I said, having been unsure if she was here or at home, but a gut feeling said she was here.

I pushed open the car door. A horrible mistake that really hurt my right shoulder. I need to be more wary; I push the door open with my left hand this time then step out, Kane following suit with his own gun in hand.

"Let's be quick but careful," I told him, heading to the front door. I wanted nothing more than to rush in, but we couldn't be careless. We don't know how many people are in there and what they are armed with, and we can't help Poppy if we end up dead.

Kane took the lead as we cautiously entered the lobby, finding the room empty.

"Where. ." Kane started, but I nudged his shoulder, silencing him.

"Keep alert, watch your back," I whispered to him. Scanning the room, I stepped forward.

The Boss's office is shut tight and the doors at the other wall that leads to the hall are pushed open. She has to be down there.

"I will take the lead. You keep an eye on our backs," I told him, walking forward before he could protest.

I have more experience doing these, and I have no time to train him right now.

The steady walk to the doors was quiet but quick. A cold wind hit me as I peeked into the hall, causing me to shiver. Why was it so cold back here?

I walk into the hall, finding the office to the left empty, and so are the cells. The window into Poppy's office showed nothing but destruction.

All her work is torn up and thrown around the room, her microscopes broken, vials shattered, and papers shredded. Whoever did this didn't want what she found to get out.

I turned back to make sure Kane followed, startled at just how close he was

"You okay?" he whispered

"yeah, I just didn't expect you to be standing so close," I told him

"Sorry," he apologized, giving me some room

"Don't be. You're just quiet," I comment, turning my attention to the end of the hall where the morgue was.

"Do you think she's down there?" Kane asked

"We have to check," I replied, walking down the hall and stopping at the door to my right. There was a small area where the elevator was, so it would be possible to transfer bodies, but for now, I would rather use the stairs.

Looking down at my only hand, which still held my gun, I signaled for Kane to open the door. When he did, a chill of cold air trickled through my skin, causing goosebumps to form. Kane gripped my left arm.

"let me go first," he spoke.

I shake him off. "You stay behind me and support me, okay?" I told him, and he didn't argue, so I kept going.

The stairs to the morgue were steep and complained under our weight. Any chance of a quiet approach is gone.

Halfway down, I paused when I heard a muffled noise. I listened for a second, making sure no one was nearby, but it sounded like Poppy pleading for help for only a brief moment. She must have something over her mouth, which meant she might not be alone.

I grip my gun and glance at Kane, who gives me an unsure glance. We were too close to the door to speak, so I just lifted my gun and stepped forward again, hoping he understood.

The door at the bottom of the stairs was closed, so when I got to the bottom, I settled beside it with Kane beside me, his shoulder brushing against my left due to the cramped space. Poppy's muffled pleas were louder, so I pressed my right ear to the door to listen for anything else, but Poppy was all I could hear.

Were they waiting for us? Or did they simply leave her down here?

I looked over at Kane who was watching me for instructions and knew we had to move so I shifted to give Kane some room so he could open the door, my gun lifted and ready for any dangers. He pushed the door slowly open. A small stream of light came through from the single light that hung in the other room, creating a slight glare. I pushed the door further open so I could see clearly inside, only to be struck with the scent of copper. The scene unfolding before me caused my stomach to twist, threatening to empty.

The drawers where the bodies go into at the end of the room were ordinary, besides an open one in the middle where I can only presume it was Coby. Oh god, he was unrecognizable.

Something that looked like a tree had sprouted from his chest. His ribs popped out, and guts scattered across the floor due to the thing that had sprouted from him. Its red trunk-like flesh extended to the ceiling while pulsating vines extended from it, covering the ceiling and traveling across the room's walls. His feet had bones sticking out at the bottom, twisted and curved like roots.

"Mill," Kane choked out, grabbing hold of my shirt, and I didn't blame him for being scared. The sight forced my heart to pound when Kane spoke my name again, shaking my right shoulder.

"What?" I asked, facing him. The door was in front of me now, but he was facing away from me, staring to the right with wide eyes, so I turned to see what he was staring at. My heart went into overdrive, my heartbeat in my ears as I saw where Poppy had gone. The shock of seeing Coby had made me forget why we even came down here, her muffled cries having gone silent, and I see why now.

She's against the wall. The vines from the tree-looking thing coming from Coby kept her in place, her feet hanging off the floor, her chest moving, and her eyes wide, which meant she was alive. Still, one of the vines had slithered down her throat, forming a bulge against her throat. I have no idea how she's not choking.

Unable to stand seeing her like this, I stepped forward, gripping the vine with my left hand, and pulled, but it didn't budge. The stupid thing did not let up as it slithered like a snake further inside of her. It didn't matter how tight I made my grip. The vine was covered with a very slippery liquid, making it nearly impossible for me to get a good grip.

"What are we going to do!?" Kane asked

"Let me think," I snapped back, sweat forming on my forehead. When did it get so warm in here? I wiped some of the sweat off my face and looked around the room, desperately trying to find some way to free her, when an idea came to mind.

"Kane, do we have a pocket knife of some sort?" I asked him,

"Uhh," he checked his pockets frantically, pulling out a cheap multi-tool. "This is all I got."

"It's good enough," I said, taking the multi-tool and popping one of the small knives out; it looked weak, but it had to work.

I pressed the blade against the vine that had forced its way down her throat and started to cut it. The first slice caused a stream of blood to erupt, staining my new clothing as some splattered across my face, but I didn't stop.

I hurriedly sliced the blade against the vine. The cuts were minor, but the vine wasn't very solid on its own, so it didn't take me much time to cut it off entirely from the primary source. The vine end spewed blood and whipped around widely like an injured animal.

"Help me pull this," I tell Kane, grabbing at the vine end and starting to pull it. The stupid thing is still resisting, but when Kane took hold of it, we were able to move it inch by inch.

Poppy let out a muffled whimper as we pulled, but we didn't stop. We had to get this thing out of her.

It was slow, but we could finally pull the vine out of her; Kane threw it across the room, and Poppy spattered, coughing violently.

"Poppy!" I spoke, putting my hand on her cheek, trying to provide her some form of comfort, but her skin... her cheek was squishy like puddy, my hand leaving an imprint.

"Thank you," she whispered, her voice strained.

"We'll get you out of here," I tell her, motioning for Kane to help me, I start to cut one of the vines holding her right arm, and Kane moves to grab her shoulders so she won't fall but. . . his hands pressed right into her skin as it fell apart causing him to stumble forward into the wall behind her... through her shoulders, her skin falling away as we saw no sign of bones.

Poppy let out a scream of pain, and Kane backed away, his face pale, fragments of her skin still on his shaking hands.

I could only look in horror, frozen by the sight the skin still around her shoulders started to peel downward, dropping to the floor in chunks, which started a chain reaction, along with her chest, then her neck, until her very head just stripped into pieces falling to the floor into a pile of nothing but flesh.

Her organs, bones, everything were gone. She was just a meat pile, yet she had screamed until her head disappeared.

I felt suddenly ill, puking onto the floor; I'd never been this disgusted by something in my life. I thought I was going to die right there.

"Mill," Kane's voice came out strained

I turn to him, wiping my mouth

"What do I do?" he pleaded, still holding his hands up. Pieces of what was once Poppy still clung to them as they shook.

I was feeling numb by everything I saw, pretty sure I was in shock, but still, I stepped over to him and wiped the skin off of him; it was all I could think of at the time.

Kane just stared at his hands, and we stood in silence. In shock by what we had witnessed, I caught a glimpse of the vines moving along the walls, slow but steady.

They were making their way towards us. The thought of becoming a pile of meat twisted my guts, so I dropped my gun into the lower pocket of my cargo pants, then gripped Kane tightly around the wrist and pulled him to the stairs. There was nothing we could do down here; Poppy was gone, and we knew nothing about those vines or what had happened to Coby.

My whole body was numb, my legs moving on their own, pulling Kane up the stairs to get out of that hell hole and didn't stop until we were at the top back in the hallway.

I turned to look down the stairs, catching a glimpse of two vines coming into view; it was traveling up here, so I slammed the door tight, my heart in my ears.

"What do we do?" Kane asked as if I could possibly know what to do, but turning to face him, I could see the fear in his eyes, which calmed me down. I had to be strong for him.

"I don't know, to be honest, but. . . We'll figure this out." I tried to reassure him, a lie I told myself. We couldn't possibly fight against something like that, but I couldn't say that out loud.

"Let's get out of here and try to call someone," I told him, explaining that we had to warn the others about this. Kane nodded, so we went down the hallway and into the lobby.

The room's silence is numbing; I couldn't stop glancing back behind us as we made our way to the front doors. I couldn't feel safe knowing what horrors lay under the station.

As we stepped outside, everything seemed so normal, Kane's car parked where we had left it, birds singing off in the distance. How would this town handle the news of whatever happened down there getting out? We can't let them know, could we? It would put everyone into a panic.

"I can't get a hold of anyone," Kane says, his phone in his hands.

"I couldn't either earlier. What is going on?" I said, looking around. None of their cars were there. Were they handling another murder? Scarlet always answers through...

I pulled my phone out of my pocket, the gun's weight still in its pocket, but for now, I ignored it. Going through the menu, I tried Scarlet again. After a few rings, it finally connected.

"Scarlet?!" I asked Kane, moving to stand by me

"Mill? Where have you been?"

"I'm at the station! Where are you guys?!"

"Listen, Mill, you must get away from the station!"

"But Poppy. . ."

"Do as I say, is Kane with you? Don't separate. Get as far away from the station as you can."

"You're not making any sense, Scarlet!" I told her

"Some. . . Awful things have happened, and they are targeting you and Kane next."

"Where are you?" I asked

"Listen, I only have a few minutes here, please, Mill. You may be our only help in regaining this town. Stay safe and don't trust anyone, okay?"

"Scarlet, please, I can't help if I don't. . ."

"GO! Damnit Mill, why are you so fucking stubborn? Just listen to me!"

I flinch. Scarlet had never yelled at me before, making this situation more terrifying.

"Okay. . But I don't know what to do."

"I trust that between you and Kane, you'll figure it out. Now, please hide."

The line cuts off, leaving the two of us in silence.

"I'm scared, Mill." Kane said.

"It'll be okay, Kane. Come on, let's get back to my place."

"Who are we hiding from?" he asked, following me to his car

"You know as much as I do. For now, we have to suspect everyone."

"And if they are at your home already?"

"They would get a face full of lead if they touched my cat," I replied, sitting on the passenger seat and composing myself. Still, after the events that had unfolded, my left hand wouldn't stop shaking.

11

The cold water from the bathroom sink sent shivers down my spine when I splashed my face; we got to my place about twenty minutes ago. Marshmellow had just quieted down a few minutes ago after she got some food, and Kane is packing a bag of food and water.

After Scarlet's warning, we agreed we couldn't stay here. It'll be too obvious of a place, so we plan to pack up and get out of here as quickly as possible.

We don't have a solid plan yet, but getting out of town and getting help from outside officers would probably be our best bet. We've tried calling about anyone we could, but the service is just dead. We are in a blackout. 911 wouldn't even work, and my TV would only show a blank image.

I have no idea how we contacted Scarlet before because her number just goes into voicemail like everyone else's.

A knock on the bathroom door startled me a little, but only briefly. Knowing it was most likely Kane, I turned off the water and opened the door.

A typical black bag held in his hands, Marshmellow rubbing against his legs, but when she spotted me, she quickly rubbed against me.

"Are you feeling better?" Kane asked

"Yeah, I do. Are we ready?"

"As ready as we can be. You don't exactly have a lot, but we should be good for driving out of town."

"Good, let's get out of here," I told him, walking to my front door. I had changed earlier, wearing my usual blue jeans and a gray button-up shirt, my gun holstered to my hip.

I take my long overcoat and slip it on along with my fedora, the familiarity of it calming me slightly, but it didn't last long. Slipping my last shoe on, I hear a knock on the front door, causing me to freeze in place and stare at it as if the door was going to come to life and eat me.

When another knock on the door came louder this time, Kane and I exchanged no words.

"I know you're here, Mill." It sounded like Benny, his voice deeper than usual.

I take a step closer to the door and lock it just seconds before the knob starts to twist.

"Let me in," he growled. "You are under arrest; if you do not cooperate, we are going to use force," he threatened.

He used the term we, who else does he have with him? I turned to Kane, who is white as a ghost. He's wearing a pack on his back and he held Marshmellow against his chest, not a thought in her eyes; she would be absolutely adorable if I weren't terrified.

Three powerful pounds erupted from the door, shaking the house

"You have a count of ten to open this door," his voice booming.

I step away from the door, goosebumps trickling against my skin, and make my way to the living room. The sliding door closed, and I didn't see anyone, so I signaled Kane to follow me.

"What are we going to do?" Kane whispered

"We have to flee," I replied, pulling the wooden bar from the door and sliding it open. An uneasy feeling washed over me, but I ignored it and stepped outside.

"You can't get away so easily!" It sounded like Debbie. I turned to my left to see her through a window, but she wore a mask to hide her face. She looked like a bobcat mixed with a coyote. It was so realistic, but the gun in her hand was what drew most of my attention.

"You don't need to do this," I told her.

"You're so ignorant," she spat, lifting her gun just as she shot. Kane pushed me out of the way, causing me to stumble. Looking back at him quickly, a streak of blood scraped his cheek.

"I'm okay," he breathed out, Marshmellow squirming in his arms as he tried to keep her restrained.

"You bastard," I growled at Debbie, pulling my own gun out

"I'm not going to miss next time," Debbie told me, lining her weapon up. Though she seemed to struggle to aim, the mask must not have good visibility. I can use this to my advantage.

"I don't miss," I replied snarkily, a pit of anger boiling in my gut due to the injury Kane had received. Be it small, I don't care. No one harms my partner without repercussion. I draw my gun and make one swift motion to aim; the trigger is easy for me to pull. I strike her gun hand, blowing it into pieces; she screams out in pain, falling to the ground.

Her scream would most likely alert Benny and whoever else was with them, so I frantically looked around. We had to get somewhere safe, but we were surrounded by the forest.

"We have to go in the woods," I tell Kane

"But we might get lost," he spoke

"We don't have much of a choice. We're sitting ducks in here!"

A bullet whistled overhead, striking my hat and blowing it off my head; I gasped and dropped to a knee, a ringing in my ears from the close call.

Kane tugged my right sleeve, forcing me back up. "We need to go," he urgently said.

I didn't want to run away, turning towards where Debbie lay in pain was a figure; he wore a mask similar to hers but a wolf with sewn-in bunny ears.

I pull my arm from Kane and shoot at the figure, taking out the right bunny ear, though they don't even flinch, firing back with surprising speed, the bullet grazing my right ear. I couldn't help but gasp, stumbling back from shock this time when Kane pulled on my right arm; I didn't fight back.

We had just got to the edge of the forest when a bullet struck a tree beside us, so I turned only to spot a third person in a bear mask. I realized we may be outnumbered. Kane's tug on my arm forced me back and I followed him, bullets flying past us as we ran together, grazing my pant leg causing another scratch, and I saw Kane get grazed on the left arm.

They were relentless as if they were a large group. Though not a single bullet struck anything significant, it was almost as if it was on purpose with how many times we had been grazed.

Regardless, we kept running. Kane led me further into the woods long after the bullets had stopped. The trees became thick, with large roots growing from the ground, but we kept trying to run, trying to put as much distance between us and those who wanted to shoot at us.

As we kept running, the ground became sloshy and wet. The slickness of the roots made it impossible to step on, so we were forced to slow down to a walk.

"I think they stopped chasing us," Kane commented.

"They chased us pretty deep into the woods," I replied, looking back, unable to see my house anymore. "Maybe we should stop and make camp for now before it gets dark?" I suggest

"What if they find us, though?" Kane asked, Marshmellow still held in his arm. She was surprisingly calm.

"Well, we can't wander around in the dark."

"Did we fail?" Kane asked. "I feel like the whole town is against us."

"As long as we are alive, we haven't lost; we'll save the town. We just. . . We just have to get out of these woods."

Kane looked away from me, silence falling over us before he turned back. "You're right; let's find a place to make camp and get some rest.

I'm sure we will find a way out tomorrow,"

I smiled. "That's the attitude," I said, stepping forward to give Marshmellow a pet. "Let's move further and find a safe area to camp."

"Okay," Kane said, turning to walk.

I followed beside him. Scanning the area for a safe spot, we could lay a camp down. The forest was thick with flora though, from prickly to soft, and some of the plants were growing taller than me even while roots poked from the ground, threatening to trip us.

If our town and lives weren't being threatened, this would almost be a nice little nature walk. My injured shoulder would ideally be gone, but at least the pain is manageable as long as I keep it still in the sling.

"Do you hear that?" Kane suddenly asked as he stepped over a root, and I followed suit

"Hear what?" I asked, looking around for any sounds

"it sounds like a gust of wind is coming our way," he replied

I stepped closer to him, placing my left hand on his shoulder just as a gust of wind washed over us, leaves rustling as I shut my eyes; Kane stumbled a little, which caused me to fall back onto my ass, expecting to fall onto the ground but instead, I felt a cold rush of water hit my back the shock of it caused me to fall entirely, my head dunking under the water, instantly sitting up and gasping for air.

I quickly wiped my now-stinging eyes before I could open them. Finding myself sitting in dark-colored water, a rotting egg smell insulting my senses as I realized Kane and I were in the middle of a swamp.

Birch trees growing from the water are scattered with vines hanging down. What appear to be massive lily pads float across the water too far for us to get a good look at.

"Are you okay?" Kane asked, both arms holding onto Marshmellow tightly so she wouldn't fall into the water.

"I might have contracted some disease, but I'm alive," I tell him, grunting as I get onto my feet.

The water went up to my knees, which I guess was something. At least we weren't in a deep lake, but damn did it smell. The water was so brown I couldn't imagine what the floor looked like.

"Do you see any land?" I asked Kane, blinking my eyes a few times. They still stung a little from falling into the water.

"No, it's all water in all directions."

"Damn," I spoke, trying to wrap my mind around this ridiculous situation. I turned to Kane, who, with wide eyes, looked petrified.

"We'll get this figured out," I attempted to reassure him

"Mill, the whole landscape changed in a blink of an eye, and we were more lost than ever. How will we figure this out?!"

that was fair. He had every right to be freaking out; hell, I was freaking out too, but I felt a sense I had to keep it together for Kane, to be strong for the both of us.

"We should start moving. We can't see land now, but maybe if we head forward, we could find some; this swamp can't go on forever."

Kane nodded slowly as he focused ahead. "Yeah, you're right. Let's get going."

"Stay close," I tell him, moving forward, the knee-high water pushing back against my legs, making our movements slower.

"I really hope we find land before we get too tired," Kane said

"I'm sure we will find some," I told him. Though I wasn't sure myself, we had to keep trying though. The townspeople were in danger.

"Hey, Mill, we're approaching one of those lily pads."

I turned to my left to face him. The lily pad was still a little ways away, but we were going to walk right beside it.

These things were huge. I've seen lily pads before, but they were never bigger than a dinner plate. But I could almost sit on this thing, and it looked as if it could support my weight, which was tempting to try, but I didn't want to risk falling back into the water. My eyes just stopped stinging, and my injured arm was still aching from the fall.

We kept trudging through the water, the lily pad coming into view a few feet from us, a strange red hue over the dark green.

"I've never seen a red lily pad before," I said curiously, stepping closer. Little blue strips ran across it, reminding me of an arm's veins, but that would be... Is it pulsating? I looked closer. The texture of the damn thing somewhat looked like hamburger meat; reaching my left hand out to touch it, the surface sticky and slimy, pulling back when I felt a pulse under the layer.

"This thing is freaking me out," I said, striding away from it, my foot stepping on something rounded and rough, almost causing me to fall but thank god I caught myself, turning around to face Kane.

"Careful, there's something in the water," I warned him

"Oh, thanks," Kane replied as he carefully waded in the water over to me, stepping over the thing I had stumbled over.

"At least if we get hungry, we can have lily pad meat," Kane joked

"I don't ever want to hear those words come out of your mouth ever again," I said. The thought of eating that thing made my stomach twist.

"Sorry, I'm just tired, too. . ." he didn't get to finish his sentence as he tripped over something in the dark-colored water even after being careful, the splash of his fall hitting me, causing me to jerk back a little to prevent my injured shoulder from getting contact again but this only caused me to slip falling backward onto the meat colored lilypad the damn thing flipping from my weight. I plunge into the water a second time.

I don't know if this was life trying to tell me something, but as I sat up gasping from the awful smell and burning eyes, I felt a little discouraged.

"Fuck!" Kane yelled, having shot out of the water. Marshmellow clinging to his chest, her soft white fur wet and sticking to her body, making her look small.

"I think this forest hates us," I said before standing up; damn, my shoulder was starting to hurt bad.

"I don't think you're wrong," Kane responded. "do you think this smell will ever come off of us?" he asked.

"We're going to smell like rotting eggs for the rest of our lives," I said dramatically, turning to the lilypad that had failed to hold me. The bottom of it looked stringy and pulsated; a weird tube-like thing came out from the middle part and bent downwards into the water. It appeared clear as water filtered through it, reminding me of a straw.

"I'm going to be sick," Kane said suddenly.

"For the love of god, please don't," I told him, turning his way; he did look pretty pale. "Are you okay?" I asked

"I think I'm going to die. I accidentally got some of the water in my mouth."

"we'll get tested for worms after this is over," I tell him

"I think I might need more than just that."

"You should be fine if you don't drink too much." I tried to reassure him even though I wasn't sure myself, I wouldn't doubt this water would have some kind of illness, getting clean and a doctor's visit wouldn't be a bad idea after this.

"You're way too calm about this situation," Kane spoke, both hands holding Marshmallow close while the bag of our supplies rested on his back, soaking wet now.

"I'm not calm, to be honest with you. I just don't show it."

"Well, I'm freaking out," Kane said. "I wish this world made sense!"

"Yeah. . . I wish for that, too," I replied, eyeing the lily pad when Kane gasped loudly.

"Snake!" he shouted

"What?!" I exclaimed, turning to follow his gaze across the water, but I saw nothing. "Snake?" I questioned.

"I saw something in the water over there; it was long and moved across the water."

Dammit, a fucking snake was the last thing I wanted to deal with. I don't think snakes in Minnesota get that big, but at this point, if you told me a boa was in these waters, I wouldn't be too surprised though I would definitely not be able to fight one of those suckers off.

"Maybe you just saw a log?" I suggested

"No, it was moving!" Kane said, his breathing quick and shallow

"Hey, it'll be okay if it is a snake; it'll be more scared of us than we are of it."

"I'm pretty sure we look like some tasty meals," Kane said

"There's two of us; animals normally avoid groups," I tell him

"Is that true?" he asked

"I honestly don't know. "I admitted, my knowledge of snakes was pretty limited. When I say limited, I mean I can identify a snake by its color scales, but whether or not it's venomous, I just avoid them to not find out.

Suddenly, off in the distance, a bellow sounded

"What the hell was that?" Kane asked

"It sounded like an elk," I replied, looking around but seeing no sign. "I don't think elk are known to live in places like this, though."

"Do you think the snake got it?!' Kane began to panic

"If a snake could swallow an elk whole, I would be concerned," I replied. But I doubt it. It didn't sound like it was in distress; "I think elk make that bellow noise normally." I tell him.

"I wonder if it's stuck in the water like us," he said

"Wouldn't that be something" I replied, looking off into the horizon. An eerie fog started to roll in, covering the swamp like a blanket; I stepped backward and pressed my back against Kane's, so I would know exactly where he was.

The elk bellowed again, though this time closer to the fog, making it impossible to pinpoint as the noise seemed to echo all around us.

Back to back, the three of us, counting Marshmellow, stood in silence, almost as if waiting for something to happen. I imagined a snake slithering at us to swallow us whole, and that would just be it. The end of our stories, no one would ever know what had happened to us.

A light in the water draws my attention, so I squint my eyes, trying to see through the fog. But my eyes didn't deceive me. A light blue glow breaks through the fog, moving slowly and stretching long, similar to a snake.

"Hey Kane, what's your knowledge on glowing animals?" I asked him,

"Uhh, plankton can glow. And some fish? Why?"

"Look," I told him, pointing to the glowing mass in the distance.

Water moved around me as Kane shifted to stand beside me

"Woah, it's almost pretty in its own way," he commented

"I can see that, but I am concerned it's getting closer," I told him

"Should we, like, run?"

"And go where?" I questioned, "The fog would make us even more lost than we already are."

Kane didn't say anything, causing silence to wash over us. We stood side by side and watched the strange glowing light drift across the water until it quickly dipped into the water, disappearing.

"Oh my god, it is a snake," Kane gasped, pressing his left shoulder into my right, almost knocking me over.

"Calm down; it's not a snake. Probably just a fish."

"How is that any better?!"

"Uh, less murdery?"

"Was that supposed to be a joke?" Kane asked

"No, I just. . ." I didn't get a chance to finish my sentence when the water around us started bubbling. The same light blue glow erupted from the water, circling us. Kane pressed his back into mine, holding Marshmellow tightly so we could watch each other's back. The glowing thing in the water moved below the surface for a few moments, then something broke the surface to my right.

Turning my head, a skull of what appeared to be an elk emerged, as white as a skull could be as if the creature had been dead for a very long time. Its eyes hollowed out while a black sludge seeped out from the sockets, little glowing blue rocks mixed in with the sludge, which I suppose is what caused the glow in the water. The elk's skull lifted upward, its jaw swinging open to reveal two long fangs. As it lifted further out of the water, black sludge with blue, glowing rocks scattered about, forming a spine and body, and thin legs disappearing into the water. The creature towered over the two of us now.

The only bones it seemed to have were a right ribcage and hip; its left front leg had a bone, too; the rest of it was sludge. A sweet honey-like smell filled the air around us as I tried to decipher what the hell this thing was.

The thing seemed to watch us even though sludge seeped from its eyes into the water. Standing on four legs, the beast's tail hung down into the water, fur growing along the back of it. The skull's head tilted, and the jaw shifted as if loose, hanging by a thread, when suddenly a yellow glow formed in both its eyes like two balls of light.

"You two look lost," a warm, soothing voice echoed from the skull, almost as if nothing could go wrong. But looking at the beast that had spoken, I couldn't help but feel frozen in fear; despite its calm voice, I didn't know what it was capable of, so Kane and I stood in silence.

"I am not going to hurt you," it told us, lowering its head low so it didn't tower over us. "I am here to help."

I flinched when it had moved, Kane's hand gripping my jacket tightly

"Am I too disgusting?" they asked us, lifting it's head up and watching the two of us with the yellow orbs.

That was a question I wasn't expecting. What do you say to a horrifying elk monster that suddenly asks if it is disgusting? I almost felt bad for it. Maybe they weren't harmful? It sure was terrifying, but it hasn't shown any form of aggression, at least yet.

I turn to Kane, who looks back at me and shrugs. Marshmellow is perched on his left arm. Turning back to the elk, I gulp.

"You're not disgusting," I told them. "We just have never encountered anyone like you before."

"Wait, are you two humans?" it asked, tilting its skull. The jaw fell off into the water, not seeming to faze it.

"of course we are; what did you think we were?"

"I get a lot of fae or elves through here."

"elves exist?" Kane asked suddenly

the creature gave a soft nod. "A lot of creatures exist in this world, normally hidden away within the veil, but there has been a disturbance, and it's fading away, blending our worlds; you two just standing here is proof enough."

"What do you mean by that?" I asked the creature, having piqued my interest.

"All over the world, forests like this one house all kinds of things like myself, but lately, I've noticed the veil that keeps us hidden from your world is growing thinner, letting humans in and even letting things out."

"Is that what is happening to Northwood?" Kane asked

"Northwood? That is the town you came from, no? There is word of a powerful entity escaping the forest. It must have infected your town."

"What sort of entity?" I asked the creature, determined to get answers to save the town.

"Oh, this happened a long, long time ago. You see, this forest is alive, much like us. I'm sure you've noticed some strange things." It moves us around as it pleases.

I bite my lip, looking at the creature. This all sounded unbelievable, but this knowledge flipped everything I believed upside down. The stories of monsters at night–is this the project of things just slipping through the cracks into our world? Marge–was she not as ill as we believed? She was sick, but all those things she had seen in the forest could have been real.

"The issue back in Northwood is people we have known for years suddenly turned on the town, or I suppose they have always turned but are just now making their move. A lot of people have died," I told the creature.

"That's the work of the entity. I get word from the gnomes in passing since they can come and go as they please, and they have mentioned a monster that goes by the name Qui Furatur Pellis."

"That's a mouthful," Kane said

"It translates to skin stealer, which is misleading; this thing is a sort of demon made centuries ago due to a cult, and well, it escaped, influencing your town to gain its powers again. I'm sure once it gets enough sacrifices and followers, it'll become pretty powerful even in the human world."

"What sort of things could it do?" I asked the creature. At this point, my legs up to my hips were growing numb, and the pain in my arm was becoming more intense. Still, this thing had valuable information I couldn't pass up the opportunity to get.

"I don't know the specifics; the gnomes would know you could always ask them."

"You've mentioned them before; how does one find a gnome?" I asked

"Look for large mushrooms. It's how they hide."

I nodded, looking at the beast, remembering that strange mushroom at home. I wonder

"Do you know how we could take Northwood back before any more innocent people die?"

There was a short pause, and the creature looked up at the sky and then back at me. "Why don't I get you out of the water? Then I will explain more."

"I suppose that would be nice," I said, unsure how this elk creature would get us to land when suddenly it disappeared into the water.

The glowing blue turned yellow, similar to its eyes, the shadow below the surface of the water swirling around until it emerged again.

This time, though, massive moose-like antlers adorn its now furred body. The creature is a mix of animals, with orange spots scattered along its stretched neck and black faded zebra stripes along its body. Its tail is fluffy and white like a fox, while bones poke out from its ribcage, neck, and hips. Its whole jaw is still white as a skull. The sludge residing in the water covers its legs.

"You may call me Dux," they said, their jaws staying still as they spoke in a soothing voice.

"It's a pleasure, Dux. I'm Mill, and this is my partner Kane," I told them. Marshmellow then meowed. "Oh, this is Marshmellow," I added, smiling at her.

Dux tilted their head. "what a cute little creature," Marshmellow meowed again, and Dux shook their head. "I see."

"You can understand her?" I asked

"Of course, are you unable to?"

"No, I adopted her, but can't understand what she says."

"How cute," Dux said, leaning their head down to look at Marshmellow. The smell of honey was intoxicated; they touched the little bell on her collar with their snout, making it ring three times. Marshmellow's pupils grew in size as she blinked a few times before looking at me.

"Mill?" She spoke in a delicate voice

"Marshmellow?!" I asked, shocked. "Did you just speak?" brushing my left hand over her head, she purred.

"I gifted her the ability to speak to you as long as she wears that collar," Dux explained.

I couldn't help but feel emotional. She is my best friend and the fact I could speak to her now... "Do you enjoy living with me?" I couldn't help but ask

"Of course, you take such good care of me," she told me, swaying her tail. "I wish we were home now."

"I know, don't worry, we will again," I reassured her

"This is insane," Kane spoke up, holding her still in his arms.

"It's amazing," I corrected him.

"Why don't you three get onto my back and out of the water?" Dux said, lowering their bodies halfway into the water so we could climb onto them.

"Right," I spoke, letting Kane get on them first. I climbed on behind Kane, surprised by Dux's warmth, especially against my legs which had gone nearly entirely numb by this point. I used my left hand to rest on Kane's shoulder so when Dux stood up. I didn't fall off, not interested in plunging into that disgusting water a third time.

Dux glided with ease through the water, carrying us without issue. My legs aching from having stood for so long, the numbness slowly fading due to the heat Dux radiated; I took this moment to have a quick breather and appreciate that we were still alive. Even after our worlds had been spun upside down, if more things like Dux existed, this might not be so bad of a change.

12

The landscape moved slowly around us as Dux waded through the water effortlessly, even with the three of us on their back.

The warmth he provided gave life back to me. The pain in my right shoulder did not go away, but it wasn't as terrible now that I wasn't as cold.

So much has happened in just a short amount of time. Not only did my town lose so many innocent lives, but there was this whole strange world I never knew existed.

Even if we manage to stop this demon, my life will never be the same. I will never be able to forget what I have seen and learned. Will I still be able to work as a detective? Things used to be so simple and mysteries were easy and predictable.

But if demons can pull people together to do hideous acts, what else would I encounter? Maybe I'll become a better detective with this knowledge; perhaps I can learn to be more open-minded.

Biting my cheek hard enough to taste copper, glancing at my left palm. The tattooed eye was still there, as perfect as I remembered seeing it for the first time.

I will have to find a way to get rid of that spirit, or I fear I may end up trapped like those other souls.

One step at a time, Mill, you'll get through this. Once your town is safe, you can focus on your own problems.

"Here we go," Dux suddenly said

"Hmm?" I asked, looking ahead and realizing we were coming up to land. The trees thickened the further they went as the birch faded out into pines.

"I will drop you three here," they said, stopping right at the shore and sunk downward to their belly so we could quickly get off.

"You go first," I tell Kane. Uninterested in trying to get around him. I let him shift and slide off, landing on the ground with a thump before turning around to grab Marshmellow.

"Do you need some help?" He asked, placing Marshmellow on the ground once he was safely a few feet from us.

"Nah, I got this," I tell him moving to slide off just like him but lose my footing and fall to my ass instead.

"You okay?" Kane asked, taking my uninjured hand and helping pull me up.

"yeah, that's harder than I thought with just the one arm," I told him with a soft smile to ease his and Marshmelows concerns.

"Please be more careful," Marshmellow purred, rubbing against my leg

"I will," I say, giving her a gentle pet.

Once we were all standing on dry land, Dux rose out of the water on their thin legs, towering over us. They would terrify anyone who ran into them, but having gotten to know them, I found them to be kinder than most people I have encountered.

"I'm thankful for everything you have done for us," I tell them

Dux lowered their head to be even with me. "you don't need to thank me; I enjoy helping others."

"Well, we still appreciate it." I pause before asking, "What do we do now? Is there anything we can do?"

Dux lifted their head and looked between the three of us. "There could be something, but I cannot promise it'll be guaranteed, nor won't put your lives at risk."

"I'll do anything."

"Even if it means putting those closest to you in danger?"

I turn back at Kane and Marshmellow, I could never put them in danger, but more people will most likely die if we don't do anything.

"I got your back," Kane told me, stepping forward and placing a hand on my shoulder.

"This could be a suicide mission," I tell him

"I'm aware, but someone's got to make sure you don't die."

I smiled before looking at Marshmellow

"I can't put you in danger," I told her

"Well, you're stuck with me."

"But you're. ."

"Mill, please, I want to help," she interrupted.

I looked to Kane, who only shrugged, then turned back to her, "You will do everything I say, okay?"

"I'll follow your orders, I promise."

sighing, I looked at Dux, who patiently awaited a response. "We want to know how to save the town."

"Very well," Dux spoke. "A very long time ago, a masterful dwarf had smelted a mighty blade made with the bone of a wyrm and the blood of an old demon." They started, pausing to see our reactions.

I couldn't see Marshmellow or Kane behind me, but I probably looked confused. Hearing about these things made me feel as if I had dropped into some book.

"Wyrms are almost nonexistent, much like my species, but dwarfs are still rather common. They typically live underground, but some have adapted to living with humans, sometimes for so long that they lose many of their dwarfen aspects."

"What's the difference between dwarfs and humans?" I asked Dux.

"Well, besides having three hundred and fifty-year lifespans, they can withstand extreme heat and have pretty tough skin."

"That's pretty neat," Kane spoke.

"They are a friendly bunch if you ever happen to meet them but very much like their own space, which is why they stay hidden."

I nod. Considering this, I wanted to learn much more, but I might have to return once everyone was safe.

"What about this blade?" I asked Dux, wanting them to continue.

"Well, this blade is powerful enough to kill just about any supernatural creature, that is, if you strike them in the heart, even a demon."

"So you're saying this blade could kill the demon infecting our town? how do we get it?" I asked

"You three must form a contract with me before I can give it to you."

"What sort of contract?"

"You will only use it against those who have killed and can only use it for good."

"Of course," I spoke, "I just want to save my town."

"I know, but I cannot let any of you take it unless you form a contract with me, and only those who have are capable of wielding this blade."

"what if we break the contract?" Kane asked

"You are unable to; this is permanently binding. Do you wish to continue?"

I turned to the other two; Kane looked as determined as ever, stepping forward to stand on my left side while Marshmellow hesitated.

"You don't need to do this," I tell her.

"I want to help, though," she replied with uncertainty

"You'll help in other ways, okay?"

She looked up at me and then loafed on the ground, her tail curling against her.

"So, just you two?" Dux asked.

"Yes," I tell them

Dux simply nodded. "Hold out your hands"

I held out my left hand while Kane chose his right, both our arms side by side when Dux let out this gurgling noise like a pot overcooking with chili until they threw up black sludge over our hands, the burning quickly causing me to bring my hand close to my chest and falling to a knee, Kane let out a wheezing gasp as he fell to both his knees.

My hand burned for only a minute as a mark formed on the top of my hand like water dripping down to my fingertips; turning my hand over to inspect my palm, the eye mark I had gained from the beast when I had almost died seemed unaffected.

"Sorry for the pain," Dux started. "It's the only way to prepare yourselves; this mark allowed you to use the dagger without any. . . Side effects."

"What are the side effects?" Kane asked, standing before I did

"No need to worry yourselves. It won't have any effect on you two."

I finally stood up. Whatever pain I had felt was officially gone, as if it was never there. Sneaking a peek at Kane's hand, I saw that he had the same marking.

"Well, I'm ready for the blade," I tell Dux.

"Please take good care of it," they replied, gurgling again. Their neck pulsated back and forth like they were about to throw up, which I suppose in a sense they did.

In their last motion, a dagger covered in sludge fell onto the ground before us.

I lean forward to pick it up, a warmth emitting from the handle. Shaking it off, the entirety of it looks like bone, reminding me of an oversized shiv. The handle part and the blade had no barrier, while red veins pulsed through it. If I hold it tight enough, I can feel the pulsating against my hand, causing my fingers to tingle.

"Thank you for everything, Dux."

"It's a pleasure; it has been a long while since I've had company. Stay well, my friends. I hope we meet again."

"Same to you," I replied. With that, Dux stepped back into the water and sunk downward, disappearing into the murky coloration. We were alone once again; we were better prepared but still alone.

The weight of the blade felt heavy in my hand, as if the expectations were trying to hold me down. It was a lot to take on, but I was thankful to have some support. I slipped the blade against my belt and pants to securely keep it in place and then turned to the other two,

"Wait, how do we get out?" I asked.

"We never asked," Marshmellow said

"Shit," Kane facepalms

"I guess we walk?" I suggest looking into the woods

"We have no other choice but should we make camp?" Kane asked

"Maybe?" I replied, looking up at the sky, the sun still high.

"Maybe I could be of assistance," a male voice suddenly said to my right. Upon facing that direction, I saw a 3-foot man with a large blue mushroom hat on his head. He wore blue overalls and was barefoot with a scruffy-looking beard. His eyes were deep ocean blue, while his beard was blond.

"My names Stickz."

13

"Stickz?" I asked, looking at the very short, slightly rounded man. His mushroom hat seemed so real that from a distance, I probably wouldn't be able to tell that it wasn't.

"Don't wear my name out now; I heard you two need to get out of these woods?"

"We do," I tell him

"Well. . I am willing to give you bunch a little help if you are willing to scratch my back," Stickz spoke.

"What are you wanting?" I asked, raising an eyebrow

"I want sugar."

"Sugar?" Kane chimed in, questioning him.

"Yes! but not any kind! I don't want to be cheaped out on you hear?! I want a big bag of it, the largest you have!"

Kane, Marshmellow, and I exchanged looks before I looked back at Stickz

"That wouldn't be an issue. We don't exactly have any on us right now, but we can get you some when we are back in town," I offered

"That's fine; you better not forget though, us gnomes are not forgiving when it comes to broken promises."

"So you're a gnome?" I asked

"Of course long legs, what else would I be? An elf?!" he burst into a hardy laugh as if he had made the funniest joke of all time.

"Uh, you can call me Mill, and this is Kane and Marshmellow," I introduced us.

"No need long legs; once our deal is done, I won't remember any of you anyway."

"Well, again, we don't have any at the moment."

"Just make sure you get it; I'll find you!"

I exchanged looks with Marshmallow and Kane, who looked equally confused.

"Well, we don't have all day, do we? Let's get a move on." Stickz suddenly announced and turned on a heel, walking away from us. Not wanting to get lost again, the three of us followed him.

The thick trees made the trek a little tricky. While Kane and I clumsily stepped over lifted roots, the gnome and Marshmellow strode through them easily.

"So Stickz," I spoke, "are there a lot of gnomes living around Northwood?"

"Oh, there are gnomes all over the world," he replied. "Besides humans, we are about as common."

"I don't remember ever meeting a gnome before now, though?"

"Well, we are everywhere, but we stay hidden away, either in the forests or nestled down in the ground, our mushroom hats the perfect disguise; you've seen me plenty of times."

I mentally facepalmed. I should have recognized his stupid hat. "So you've hung around my yard, then?" I asked; the image of that large blue mushroom that had grown in my yard came to mind; damn, I felt so stupid.

"It's sort of sad how gullible you humans are, but it's better for us, I suppose," he said, shrugging his shoulders as he continued at the same pace.

I wanted to say more, but we came to an opening, finally stepping out from the thick forest only to find ourselves at Gary's house.

"Welp, this is as far as I can go," Stickz said

'We couldn't get closer to town?" I asked him

"No, it's too dangerous to be close; sorry, this is as close as I'm able to get."

I nod, sighing a little; it was better than nothing. "Thanks, Stickz."

"Don't thank me if you both don't die. I'm coming for my bag of sugar; you better not forget."

"Don't worry, we won't."

"Good," and with that, he was gone, walking back into the woods without much of a goodbye.

"Well, at least we're out of the woods?" Kane said

"Yeah, let's go see if Gary is home," I replied, making my way to the house; I wondered how long we had been gone for; if I had been gone for two days just walking around, I couldn't imagine how many days had gone by after that long journey. Man, my legs ached, and I smelled awful, not to mention the constant pain in my shoulder.

The grass grew past our ankles, wetting the bottom of my stiff pants. I can't wait to change out of these things. I wonder if Gary has some extra clothing we could borrow.

Making our way around the yard, we spotted his truck parked at the front, which meant he had to be home.

"Let's hope he doesn't mind us just dropping by," Kane said

"I'm sure he wouldn't mind," I replied, walking up the steps to his place. The familiar creaking no doubt would alert anyone we were here.

"Have I met Gary before?" Marshmallow asked

"I don't think so," I told her. "He doesn't leave his place often," I added just before knocking on the door. The three of us went quiet, but there was nothing but silence on the other end, so I knocked again, louder this time.

"Gary! it's Mill and Kane!" I loudly spoke through the door, but still, nothing.

"He hadn't gotten hurt, did he?" Marshmellow asked, walking up to the door to give it a small scratch

"I sure hope not," I replied, reaching out and testing the doorknob. It twisted, and I swung the door into a deafeningly quiet house.

"Gary?" I called out, but still, nothing, so I stepped further into the house.

I peeked into the kitchen, but everything looked completely normal: the chairs were pushed in, and the table was clean. However, a layer of dust covered everything.

"He has to be somewhere," Kane said, walking down the hall

"Stay here," I tell Marshmellow, ensuring she stays by the door before I walk into the kitchen, brushing a hand over the table, a thick coat of dust covering my finger.

"I don't think anyone's been here for a while," I spoke loudly

"He's nowhere to be seen!" Kane called out, walking into the kitchen

"Did you check upstairs?"

"No, not yet."

"Okay, let me," I tell him, walking around and putting a heavy foot on the first step. "See if you can't find anything to eat. If Gary isn't here, I don't think he'll mind."

"Isn't that stealing?" Marshmallow asked

"We'll replace whatever we eat," I replied. "We need some energy before we make the trek back into town."

"Okay, I'll look," Kane told me, walking into the kitchen, Marshmallow hesitating at the doorway.

"Stay down here with him," I told her, and with that, I started up the stairs. The back of my legs screamed, but I just pushed through.

The sounds of Kane in the kitchen messing around with things and talking with Marshmallow are nothing but noise while I stand on the top step. Gary's upstairs consists of just two rooms: a bathroom to my right and his office directly in front of me, which I have only seen once.

The office door was closed, while the bathroom was wide open, showing that it was empty. So I knocked on the office door, and upon hearing nothing, I opened it.

The small office seemed untouched for what seemed a long time. The window in the back was dirty and hard to see through. The table to the room's left housed a dead plant I can't identify anymore and an old car model. To the far right stood a wall of bookshelves filled to the brim.

My attention, though, went to the desk in the middle of the room. Cluttered with papers, a closed laptop sat in the middle. A dusty cup of water was near the back corner, and one of those bird things beside it was no longer drinking from the cup.

So I stepped forward, gently tilting the bird down so its beak touched the water, and watched it do its job, finding the little thing calming in a strange way. After I was satisfied, I sat down at the desk and looked through the papers, but most of them were reminders of his job; Gary, even though he was considered retired, he still did some work on the side as an editor.

None of it was helpful to his whereabouts, so I lifted the heavy laptop lid, and a bright light came onto a disorganized desktop.

"Damn, Gary," I mumbled. All the icons were oversized and took over the screen, the green landscape barely visible behind it all.

"Mill!" Kane called from downstairs, startling me

"Yeah!" I called out, my eyes focused on the screen, clicking around for anything important

"I have some food made up, so why don't you get some?"

"I'll be right there!" I called back. I had to find something before I could sit down.

Clicking around the desktop, I found absolutely nothing. Most were single-player games like Solitaire or chess, which you play with a computer. The rest were just drafts for work, but I couldn't use any of them, so I shut the laptop and walked to the bookshelves.

Gary was an older guy. Maybe he had a book somewhere. Most of the books were dusty, though, much like everything else, it would be a while before, wait a minute.

A book stood out on the middle shelf. It was very subtle, but unlike any of the other books, there wasn't a speck of dust on it, so of course, it piqued my interest, so I pulled it out of the shelf. The book was made of dark leather with an evergreen leather strap, keeping it closed and its quality remarkable.

I undo its leather strap and open the first page. The journal dates back to 1945. If I calculate it correctly, Gary would have been roughly 18 when he first wrote in this.

Would it be wrong of me to read this? I bite my lip, thinking it might hint at where he was, considering it wasn't dust-covered. He may have written in it before leaving.

Figuring it might be my best clue, I stepped back, sat in the chair, and flipped to a random page to read.

'In three days, I will be graduating high school. I can't wait to finish school and start my life. My mom already told me she expects only the best, but I honestly just want to stay here in Northwood. I know she expects me to go to the big city and attend an expensive college, but I'm not going... I haven't told her yet.'

Many of the first few pages were like this; it seemed Gary was under a lot of pressure from his mom, but this wasn't going to help me find him, so I skipped forward.

'Q told me it wouldn't be all bad being kicked out of my home. He even helped me find this new place. It wasn't easy, but I'm glad to have such a good friend. He told me we'll go camping sometime, which will improve my mood.'

He mentions this Q guy on some of the other pages, but it seems they get closer from here on out. I've never heard of him before, and Gary has never mentioned him. I wonder if something happened between them. I check the time on my phone. I need to hurry this up, so I skip ahead.

'what did I do? What have I done? Q told me it had to be done in order to be part of the group, but the regret had fully set in. I'm going to miss you, Whiskers. I'm sorry things ended this way; I hope I struck your heart quickly enough... I am questioning the rules Q had told me, but I'm too far in; Whisker's blood is on my hands, and I am not going to make his death vain. Tomorrow is my ritual of becoming a part of the group. I better make sure my suit is clean.'

I quickly went to the next page. I couldn't believe what I was reading. Did he really kill his cat in order to be a part of this group? Who is Q, and what is this group? There were so many questions that I decided to keep reading a little more to find out.

'My leg still hurts a lot even though it's been a week since I've been branded; Q told me I had to have it to show my devotion to the God that protects us, a God I thought was going to save my friends and me from this awful life and to give eternal life but I'm unsure if it's a religion I really want to be a part of anymore everything Q has us doing feels so wrong and Debbie feels the same though she's been branded for a year now. Mike had his ritual the same day as mine and is completely in for it. I want to leave, but they are the only reason I can afford this house and food right now, so I'm stuck until I can earn enough money. Q watches us all closely. I can't let him know how I feel, or I'll be punished, so I'll keep this journal hidden and lay low.'

It sounds like Gary got into some trouble. Flipping forward, the rest of the pages were blank, so I suppose he stopped writing altogether when a small slip of paper dropped from the book. I picked it up to find my name scribbled on it. Did Gary know I'd find this book? I set the book down and unfolded the paper to find a rashly written note.

'I don't know when or if you'll find this, but I hope it's you, Mill; by the time this book is found, I will be long gone. I made some awful mistakes in my life. The only good thing I ever did was be a dad, and even then, I fucked up. I hoped I had more time, but it seemed the so-called God I had devoted most of my life to finally become strong enough; after Q had died, I was finally free to leave. I hadn't realized the others still sacrificed to the God, and when people started turning up dead left and right, I realized they were preparing to release the damn thing... Even after I left, I had been branded, and so even in death, I will never escape the claws of the thing I once called a God. I don't think the others realized we were just pawns to be killed when the time came, so before that can happen, I will go my own way. Tell my family I love them and I am sorry for all I have done. If I had been braver, I could have done more to help, but I can't, so I'll find serenity in the fact I lived a life and gave what I could to my family.'

A twist in my stomach caused me to feel nauseous. Something this awful had been hanging over Gary's head all this time. I wish I had discovered this other side of the world. I could have helped him, though I supposed, just like him, you can't really change the past. All I can do is take this information and maybe use it to change the course of the future. I'm not letting this demon take Northwood over. I'm going to take this blade gifted to me by Dux and take it down, even if it means my death.

Suddenly, I heard someone walk up the steps, and Kane appeared in the doorway.

"I've been calling you. Is everything okay?" he asked, stepping further into the room.

"Oh, yeah, sorry, I found a journal Gary wrote in," I reply, standing up from the chair, my legs shaking a little; I slip the note back into the book and hand it over to Kane. "Take a read"

"Does this say where Gary is?"

"Not where he is, but it does confirm he won't be coming back."

"Oh..." Kane said, staring at the journal. "Well, I'll read this, but why don't you get some food in you? I found the keys to Gary's truck; we can head out once you're ready."

"That sounds nice, actually," I tell him, making my way to the doorway. "I'll eat some, then we can head out right after," I tell him, walking down the stairs.

It was tempting to shower and get some new clothing, but I was afraid of taking my sling off. My shoulder ached when I moved too quickly, and the thought of pulling it out of the sling made my skin crawl, so I'll wait until after we finish our job. I will take the longest bath ever and wash my clothing a few hundred times before I wear them again due to the smell of swamp water.

Taking a left into the kitchen, I see Marshmellow sitting on the table nibbling on some sandwich meat, not the healthiest, but I suppose for now it'll have to do; I walk to the fridge to check inside, finding some random assortments of food and settle on a sandwich Kane must have made.

"Are we leaving?" Marshmellow suddenly asked, startling me. It's going to take a while to get used to her talking.

I turned to her. "Soon, I just want to eat first," I told her, taking a bite from the sandwich and tasting something familiar. I opened it up to pull off the tomato Kane had placed in it, hating the taste.

Loud thuds come from the stairs, and then Kane emerges from the doorway. "woah, this is insane. I can't believe Gary's journal," he exclaimed

"It seems this has been going on for a long while," I reply.

"Should we go looking for him?" Kane asked, pulling a chair out and flipping it around so he could sit on it backward.

"He's already made his mind up; it'll be pointless trying to find him when we have the tool to save the town; it's best to let him be at peace."

"But we can't just let him go off and die."

"Listen, Kane, I don't like it either, but we don't know where he has gone, and we can't waste time."

"That's so cruel. . ." Kane said, slumping over the chair. Marshmellow sat silently on the table, looking between us as we spoke.

"You are more than welcome to look for him, but I'm taking his truck and heading to Northwood to deal with this demon."

Kane fell silent for a moment, and I finished up my sandwich

"I'll go with you," Kane said quietly. "You're right; we have to see this in the bigger picture. I just hope he's okay."

"Well, look at it this way: You read the journal. If we manage to kill this thing without being killed ourselves, we may save Gary in a way."

"Right. . I suppose you're right about that."

"Are we on the same page now?" I asked, walking to the table to give Marshmellow a head pat

"Yeah, I'm with you, Mill, lets head to town."

"Good," I replied, taking a deep breath. "Come on, Marshmallow. You'll lay low once we get to town, okay?"

"I will, Mill, don't worry," she replied, hopping off the table and following Kane to the front door.

I allowed myself a second to collect myself, taking in the quiet room around me. I sure hope Gary found the peace he was looking for; when this is all over, I'll come back here and look for him and call his family.

"Come on Mill!" Marshmallow called from the door, the engine of the old truck rearing up

"I'm coming," I replied, walking to the door and watching Marshmellow run back towards the truck and hop into the open passenger door.

If anything, I will do everything in my power to ensure she lives. I wish I could leave her somewhere safe, but being with me is the safest for now. At least I can watch over her along with Kane. He's so new to this, but he's done so well to keep up and be helpful. I don't think I could have asked for a better partner in this scene.

"You good Mill?" Kane asked, poking his head out from the car window

"Huh? Oh yeah, let's head to town", I tell him, walking to the truck and sitting in the passenger seat, Marshmellow curling up on my lap.

14

I suddenly awoke from an unexpected nap when Kane shook my left shoulder.

"What?! Did I fall asleep?!" I asked, startled. Marshmellow squirmed on my lap as she woke up, too.

"You did, but look," Kane spoke, his voice cracking as he pointed forward; the truck stopped just before town.

I groggily rub my eyes and look through the windshield; suddenly feeling sick, Northwood was unrecognizable.

The ground had grown skin. A fleshy pink material covered the ground and over the trees, stopping in a straight line in front of us as if there were a barrier. The skin moved softly as if it were breathing.

White specks were randomly scattered across it like puss-filled pustules.

From here I saw the outlines of the apartment building, or at least what I assume is the building; The same pink flesh stretched over it. The whole town must be covered.

"deer lord," I spoke

"How the hell are we supposed to get into Northwood with this. . . This?"

"Fleshy floor?" I asked,

"Yeah!"

"We can keep driving?" Marshmellow asked from my lap

"Do you think I could just. . . Drive over it?" Kane asked.

"I don't think we have any other choice," I replied, brushing my left hand over Marshmellow's back to help keep her calm.

"I suppose here goes nothing," He said hesitantly, then pressed the gas pedal, moving us forward.

Kane white-knuckled the steering wheel as we made our first contact with the flesh. The truck's front tires started to slip, forcing us forward with a jolt, which was game over.

We slid down the road, Kane trying to keep it under control, but whatever he did, the truck wouldn't stop. The ground slick while pieces of the flesh kicked up behind us from the tires, the truck shifted left then right as Kane tried to regain control.

When the truck spun around I held Marshmellow against my chest with my left arm. Luckily, we weren't going too fast, so it only spun once and finally stopped. Now facing the direction we had come from, Kane attempted to hit the gas again, but the truck stayed in place, kicking up the flesh behind us and only trapping us further.

"Shit," Kane said, his voice cracking.

I leaned back into the seat. "I can't tell you guys how much I don't want to step out of this car."

"I don't think we have a choice," Kane said

I sighed dramatically. "Yeah, let's get a move on. I have a feeling this short walk to town is going to take us a while," I say, sitting up and hesitantly putting my hand on the door handle.

"Can I be carried?" Marshmellow asked

"I can carry you," Kane spoke. "Come here," he added, gesturing for her to come over, scooping her into his arms.

I took in a few deep breaths and then pushed open the car door, the smell of rotting meat punching me in the face.

"Oh god," I groaned, looking down at the ground; it all looked so much worse, close-up. Little strings of veins could be seen all through it.

"How deep do you think it goes?" I asked, turning around to face Kane as he jumped out of the truck, the fleshy ground going up to his ankles.

"I think I'm going to be sick," he told me.

"Just hang in there," I replied, sliding out of the seat and trying to be as gentle as possible. When I landed, the fleshy ground squished past my shoes to my ankles, soaking my socks.

I am going to need new skin after this is all done; I feel so unclean.

"Are you okay?" Marshmellow called out. I turned and saw Kane and her through the truck's open doors.

"Yeah, just adjusting."

"let's meet behind the car," Kane said, turning and trudging towards the back of the truck closer to Northwood.

The liquid pooling in my shoes made me feel like I had dipped them into the water during the winter. I had no doubt they would be numb after a while, so before that could happen, I started to walk towards Kane.

"This is so cold," I comment

"We really need to find real ground."

"Well, let's start heading to Northwood," I tell him, turning to face the town. The fleshy ground extends for miles, so we better get used to it.

I let Kane get ahead of me so I could keep an eye on him and Marshmellow. I took one last glance at the truck, the whole front end covered in blood and flesh, looking as if we had hit an animal. Trying to clean it will be a task on its own, that is, if we manage to make Northwood normal again.

Though Who is to say that after this is done and over with, any of this would disappear?

"Mill, it's not the time to be in your head," Kane called out, and I snapped my head around; he had gotten several feet ahead of me.

"Coming!" I exclaimed, trudging through the slippery ground towards him. Whatever was past the squishy top layer felt hard. Maybe it was the true ground?

Catching up to Kane, I began walking beside him this time, the two of us awkwardly stepping forward, trying our best not to fall. This made us take forever to get to town, but once we had gotten on the road in front of the apartment building, we finally paused to take a breather.

Everything from the ground up was covered entirely in this flesh.

"If I was a cult, where would I be?" Kane asked, looking around

"The better question is, where is everyone?"

"Maybe they're all trapped in the buildings?" Kane replied

"God, I can't imagine the smell; it's already unbearable out here."

"Maybe we should keep going?" Marshmellow suggested

I take in my surroundings, trying to consider where this demon would be located; by Gary's journal, it's definitely confirmed that John and Debbie are in on this, so maybe one of their houses or maybe...

"Let's go to the downtown area," I tell the other two. "Let's see if we can find anyone."

"Are you sure it's a smart path?" Kane said

"We don't know where anyone is, so it's worth a try."

"I believe in Mill," Marshmellow said

"Thank you," I tell her, stroking her fur gently while Kane still holds her.

"Well... Okay then, let's go," Kane said.

I took the lead this time, walking and frequently sliding, scanning the area constantly as we walked. Luckily, neither of us fell as we made it downtown, where all the little shops were.

The bar stands out from the rest of the small shops, being the only thing in this whole town beside us not to be blanketed over by this flesh. I don't know why this specific building was so important, but fuck, I'm going to take it.

I pressed my left arm against the door, expecting to push it open, but all I did was run into it, smacking my face and causing me to stumble back.

"It's locked," I groaned out

"Are you okay?" Kane asked, struggling to contain a laugh

"Yeah, just wasn't expecting that," I say, looking his way, unable to help but smile. It was silly, but I'm glad he can still find some humor in all of this.

"Let's try this differently," I say, knocking on the door.

There was a rustling behind the door before it cracked open a little for someone to peek through.

"Mill?" the voice asked, opening the door more; it was Bob.

"Yeah, it's Kane and I," I tell him, relieved to see him safe.

"It's so good to see you two. I can't believe you're still alive," he replied, opening the door more so we could step inside.

The bar itself smelled of jasmine, a calmness washing over the space. Soft music played from speakers as if the outside world weren't awful. Eleven people were here, which was a big chunk of the population, though not everyone.

Wallace stood behind the desk, cleaning off the counter. His ocean-blue eyes were focused, and his hair completely shaved. He was a mysterious man with slightly pointed ears.

James, Jessy, and that new guy Zion sat at the bar, all with their drinks. Vector and Sidney sat at a booth to the right. Then there was Chloe, Scarlet, Jea, and Sam sitting around a table playing card games.

Everyone had on pajamas, their eyes tired, and they moved sluggishly.

"How long has this been going on?" I asked Bob, who stood in front of us.

"It's been a week since the town was infested, but two weeks since the cult came out and announced themselves; they had gathered everyone into the park as a town meeting. At first, the boss had set it up, and then that was where they tried to convince us to join," he explained.

"Who all was a part of it?" I asked him

"Well, besides the Boss, we saw Debbie and John then. . ." Bob paused, hesitating a moment, so Scarlet spoke up, speaking across the room

"Mike was there too."

"Oh, I'm so sorry, Bob," I tell him, but Bob only shakes his head

"I've come to terms with it. I just wish I saw it sooner. Maybe I could have stopped it from happening."

"Don't blame yourself," I tell him, turning to Scarlet and the table. Chloe owns the salon in town. Her hair is long and bright red, and she usually wears very snug-fitting dresses, so seeing her in loose blue pajamas was strange. Jae was quiet as usual, but so was Sam, which was out of character for him. He typically bothers me with answers to cases, but right now, he seems disinterested.

"Do you guys know where everyone else is?" I asked

"A lot of us got separated, so whoever isn't here, I'm not sure," Scarlet said, turning our way, bags under her eyes.

This was when Sidney stood. "They took Elton," she whimpered

"They took your child?" Kane questioned

"I couldn't stop them," Sydney cried, sitting back down while Victor comforted her.

Scarlet spoke up this time, "I've tried going out several times to find the others, but with whatever has grown over Northwood, it's nearly impossible to find anyone, and we don't have the supplies nor manpower to be efficient."

"You are all doing good with food and water?" I asked

"Yeah, Wallace has a pretty good supply."

I nod; considering this, my attention pulls to James. "How are you doing?" I asked him

"I could be better," he admitted, "but I'm alive, and Wallace makes good drinks." He added, mustering the best smile he could that didn't quite reach his eyes.

I noticed this but decided not to pry. I was thankful he was alive, though concerned for Luke. However, based on what Scarlet said, they have yet to learn where they are.

"Well, don't worry, we'll try and fix things."

"What the hell are you going to do?" Sam suddenly questioned, "You have an injury. You're worse off than most of us."

"True, my shoulders fucked up, but if we don't do anything, then nothing will be fixed; in fact, it'll all get worse."

Scarlet stepped forward this time. "What do you know?"

I turn to Kane. "Do you still have the journal?"

"Yeah," he said, setting Marshmallow down, who had been quiet this whole time, and pulled out Gary's journal.

"What's this?" Scarlet asked, taking it from Kane

"It's Gary's journal. It might not explain everything, but I want you to hold onto it and also keep an eye on Marshmellow for me."

Marshmellow imminently declined. "No! I'm coming with you."

Her soft voice echoed in the room, causing everyone to look our way in disbelief.

"Did. . . Did she talk?" Bob asked

"Yeah, so a lot has happened, and Marshmellow can speak."

James spoke up this time, "What the hell have you three been up to?!"

"It's a long story. . . I'll let Marshmallow explain it when we leave."

"I'm not staying behind!" Marshmellow argued.

"Please, I need to know you are safe," I tell her

"But. ."

"No buts," I interrupted

"You shouldn't go either," Bob told me

"I'm going regardless of what you say."

"You're going to get yourself killed."

"Then so be it."

Scarlet stopped Bob from speaking by placing a hand on his shoulder and having him step back.

"let me come with you two," she said

"Thank you, Scarlet, but I want you to stay here," I tell her

"You know I'll be helpful to you."

"You'll be amazing, but that's why I need you here; if things go wrong, you'll be the best to ensure these people stay safe."

"Things have already gone very wrong, Mill."

"Things are awful, but there is help. This fleshy stuff stops on the outskirts of town; there's a barrier. I want you to take everyone there and get out of town."

"but what about the others?" She asked

"Kane and I will do what we can, but you are here now. Get out of town. At least then, I know you'll be safe. And take Marshmellow."

Scarlet looked at me with concern, hesitating momentarily before speaking, "I'll do you proud; I'll ensure everyone leaves safe."

"I don't doubt you," I tell her, feeling guilty for leaving Marshmellow with her. I can't stand the thought of her getting hurt because of me; if there was anyone I could trust her with, it would be Scarlet.

"Are you sure about this?" Kane asked, standing by my right shoulder

"Yeah, I am," I replied, giving him a reassuring smile before turning back to Scarlet and looking down at Marshmellow. Her bright blue eyes were watching me, full of concern, so I kneeled down to brush my left hand across her fur.

"I know you want to come and help, and I'm so proud of you for having that courage, but you're my whole world, Marshmellow, and I want to protect you. So please, stay with Scarlet so I can keep protecting you."

"Do you promise you'll come back?" She asked

"I'll do everything I can to return. You have my word."

"Well, okay. . I'll hold you to that."

"You just stay with Scarlet," I tell her, standing up fully and looking around the room. I wanted to take time and say bye to everyone, but there were too many missing people, and not to forget Sydney's kidnapped child, we need to search for them.

"Do you two want some rest?" Wallace spoke, setting a glass in front of James

I turn to Kane questioningly, "I know you're tired too, but I can't rest until after this is over."

"I won't leave your side," Kane told me.

James was suddenly to my left, placing a hand on my shoulder to grab my attention.

"You're going to need rest, Mill; you are only human, and so is Kane."

"You worry too much," I tell him.

"And you worry too little," he argued back. "This isn't a case you can just solve by running out and hoping for the best, Mill."

"I can't just not do anything."

"You're going to get yourself and Kane both killed," James harshly spoke.

"Things might indeed be stacked against us, but we have a way to possibly stop this, and we have to try," I tell James, taken back by his harsh words. He's never spoken to me in that tone before, though I'll give him the benefit of the doubt, considering everything they've gone through.

James had only sighed at my words and continued to drink what Wallace had given him.

I flinched a little when I felt a hand on my right shoulder, turning to see it was Kane.

"If we want to make any progress, we should get going," he told me

"Yeah, let's get back out there."

"Should you two eat at least?" Bob asked

"We had something not long ago," I tell them, my stomach nauseous due to the flesh-covered ground. I don't think I could stomach anything quite yet.

"Wait," Wallace suddenly spoke.

I turned his way just as he walked around the counter, handing over a paper bag.

"It's a few sandwiches, just in case; come back anytime I'll be here."

"You're not going with the others?" I asked him

Wallace shook his head calmly before walking back to the bar. "I'm staying here with my bar," he said.

"It'll be best for you to go with the others."

Wallace merely shrugs, seeming to be done with the conversation. I meet eyes with Scarlet.

"I'll talk with him, don't you worry."

"Thanks, Scarlet, I'm counting on you."

"You two better not die."

"I will try," I told her before backing up and giving Kane one last glance to ensure he was doing okay. He looked scared but determined, much like me.

"Mill, wait!" Marshmellow called out just before I opened the door; she ran toward me and jumped into my arm, nuzzling my neck. "You better come back."

"For you, I will," I tell her, hugging her tightly before setting her down. "We'll be back home before you know it."

She didn't seem satisfied but backed up anyway, besides Scarlet.

"We will be back," I told them, the last thing I said before turning to face the door.

It felt weird leaving the bar like this. Everyone looked so defeated and tired, a sight I never thought I would see my fellow townspeople in. Kane and I were in no better shape. Honestly, I didn't know how we would go about all of this, but we had to try.

We were the ones with the dagger gifted by Dux, which gave us an advantage. If we didn't try, those lost in the town would not have a chance.

With my heart full, I opened the door to the bar, waving everyone off before I stepped back onto the slippery flesh-covered ground with Kane by my side. I know it was selfish, but I wanted him to be by my side. He's shown time and time again that he's capable.

"Where are we headed?" Kane asked

"To the park," I told him with false confidence

"You think we will find them there?"

"I'm not entirely sure, but Bob said that was where everyone had met up when this all started, so if anything, there'll be a clue."

"If it's not trapped under this flesh, that is"

"Let's hope not," I replied, already anxious.

For all I know, they could be off in the woods, making this impossible, but I need to stay positive; everyone is counting on us.

Taking a few clumsy steps down what was once the sidewalk, leaving the bar behind.

We'll save this town... We have to.

15

We finally made it to the road that turns to a right and will take us directly to the park. The police station in front of us matches everything else with a blanket of skin. My feet are numb from red liquid squeezing out from the ground when I apply pressure to them, and my legs are sore and achy, but I carry on turning right.

"I hope we find everyone else safe and sound," Kane spoke up

"Same," I replied, focused ahead

"I can't stop thinking about the cult," Kane said. "Do you think they knew the demon they worshiped was evil?"

"Well, in Gary's journal, he called it a god before a Demon, so I would assume that's what the others think, too. But regardless, they've killed due to it, and that's punishable."

"Yeah. . . it's just hard to think of people I've known my whole life to do something like this."

"I've seen a lot in this field, and I still wasn't prepared for any of this," I admitted.

How could we? Supernatural creatures? A goddamn demon-worshiping cult? And the ground grew its own fucking skin? No one could have been prepared for this.

"Makes you wonder what else is out there," he said

"Probably more than we can ever imagine," I replied, focusing on the ground before me; I wanted to make good time but also didn't want to fall and risk injuring myself further.

Silence fell over us as we descended the path until the park appeared. The once prosperous area was soiled by the flesh that had spread across the field and grew over the trees.

"Who is that?" Kane asked, pointing to a figure off in the distance;

from here, all we could see was a silhouette.

"Let's go find out," I replied, making my way to them, my heart pounding. Why did I suddenly feel on edge?

When we get closer, I realize I don't recognize the man. He stood roughly 5'8, had no hair on his head, and I don't think he even had eyebrows? He wore gray baggy sweatpants and a baggy yellow hoodie; I couldn't tell if he had shoes on from where I stood.

"Are you okay?" I called out to the man. He turned his head to look at us but didn't say a word, his eyes dark.

"Maybe he's hurt," Kane suggested

"I don't know; something seems off," I replied, making my way closer to the man, his pale skin tight over his skeletal body.

"Is everything okay?" I tried again. "Who are you?" I questioned.

The man squinted his eyes as if trying to piece something together before a realization crossed him.

"oh, this is interesting," he suddenly spoke, his yellow-stained teeth seemed too sharp.

"What is?" I asked the man, confused. I stopped just at the park's edge, unwilling to get closer.

"You are Mill, aren't you?" the man asked, seeming almost excited to see me. He took a few steps closer, revealing he did indeed have no shoes.

"Yes, who are you?" I asked wearily, watching him.

"You've heard of me, I do go by many names, but I prefer the one your little townsfolks call me, God," the man spoke, a sizeable smug smile crossing his lips.

"Wait your the. . ." Kane started

"The demon? Yes, I know it's disappointing not to see my true form, but this body is necessary for being out here."

I looked at this thing in disgust. "You killed the man and wore his body?" I asked

"Very skin walker of me, right? I can't quite master their skills, but I think I do pretty damn good."

I felt speechless. This was not what I expected, but I didn't know what to expect in the first place, so seeing this instead of some half-goat monstrosity... Well, it was underwhelming.

"Aren't you going to say something?" the demon asked, tilting his head and narrowing his eyes on me. "I've had my eye on you for a while now."

I raised an eyebrow. "And how is that?" I questioned, prying for more information.

"You've proven to be. . Resilient with everything I've thrown at you; not many humans can without going insane."

"You threatened my home; It's my job to keep it safe, even if it means dealing with something like you."

The demon gave out a hardy laugh. "Oh, you're delightful," he said, walking closer, about two feet from Kane and me now. He smelt like a rotting corpse.

"I want you to join me," he said

I scoffed, then, "Fuck you," I snarled

"Oh, come on, name your price. Do you want riches? Power? Just name it."

"I want you to leave this town and never return."

"You mortals always have a price; what if I bring back a loved one?"

I gritted my teeth. I would love my parents back, but I don't think the form of bringing them back would be precisely what I expected, especially from a demon.

"We don't want anything you have to offer," Kane spoke, and instantly, the demon snapped his neck towards him, anger washing over his eyes.

"I don't give a damn about you," he growled low before turning to me

"If you do not take any of my deals, I will just kill you both," he threatened.

"Well, the deals you've offered I have no interest in," I tell the demon, weighing my options. There was nothing more I wanted to do than take my dagger and strike him, but I might only get one chance at this, so I needed to make it count.

"Well, I might have a deal you'll like," he suggested, a mischievous glint in his eyes.

"Oh?" I questioned, humoring him.

"What if we play a game? You want to save this town, right? Well, if you can save everyone, then I will leave."

"And if I lose?"

"Mill, don't," Kane pleaded; I ignored him.

The demon smiled satisfyingly. "You will have to join me."

"Doesn't this counter your whole, not willing to give up control thing?" I asked

"I'm willing to gamble; I find it fun to watch mortals like you scramble," he laughed. "I'll even sweeten the deal; if you win, those who have vowed to me will be released of their bonds."

"You seem pretty cocky," I comment.

"I don't lose," the demon said, reaching a sickly hand out, "Do we have a deal?"

I look at the demon parading around as a man then down hand, how easy would it be to stab him right now, but what if this action doesn't save everyone?

I could feel Kane's grip on my left shoulder tighten. I could not guarantee this would play out fairly, so I had to do what I came here for and hope for the best.

In one swift motion, I pulled the dagger from my belt and struck the demon's hand, lounging forward to stab him; the demon moved left and grabbed my arm, then spun, sending me several feet from him.

Landing roughly against the ground, I slid a little, my whole back soaking wet now.

"Mill!" Kane screamed, so I hurriedly sat up, still dazed from being thrown, only to watch Kane get sucked down into the ground, letting out a gurgled scream as he disappeared completely.

"Kane!" I shouted, standing, but my legs were knocked from under me, causing me to faceplant the ground. Screaming out when I landed on my injured shoulder, only to end up gagging from a slimy piece of meat from the ground, causing me to choke before I coughed it up.

"tsk, tsk," the demon spoke, kneeling beside me and forcing my head down onto the ground, causing me to choke and struggle for air. Letting go just before I passed out, my vision spotting.

"Now, you are going to listen," the demon hissed, his knee against my back so I couldn't get up. "I am not going to play nice. You better take this deal, or I am going to force you to watch me tear your little partner apart, skin, organs, everything removed slowly and painfully."

"Can you force a deal?" I groaned out, still tasting that flesh in my mouth; it weirdly tasted like pork.

"I can do whatever the hell I want," he replied, applying more pressure against my back, causing pain to shoot from the spot only to be numbed out from the pain in my shoulder.

I tried to locate the knife I had used, but with my head pressed into the fleshy ground, I couldn't see it or how far it was, leaving me completely vulnerable.

"So?" the demon asked impatiently, not giving me enough time to properly think this over.

"Fine, I'll do it!" I whimpered out, blinded by the pain in my shoulder.

"Good boy," he said, grabbing the back of my shirt and forcing me onto my feet. Disoriented, I looked at him and realized he had a hand out.

"It can't be official until we shake on it," he spoke

I hesitated, attempting to look for the dagger, but he took my chin and forced me to look forward

"Focus, human; I'm starting to think you might not be as bright as I had thought."

"Fine," I grumbled, reaching my left hand out, which the demon took greedily, shaking my hand violently.

"This is going to be fun," he said, letting my hand go

"What exactly am I doing?" I questioned, realizing I should have asked before shaking his hand.

"You need to find the remaining townspeople without dying."

"Right," I spoke, "And can I have any hint?"

"Hmmm, I suppose it would only be fair, go to the high school; that's where they are, but don't think it'll be easy."

"I didn't think it would be," I told him. Glancing at my left hand, it suddenly felt itchy and dry.

"I can't wait for you to join my followers," the demon spoke with a confidence that made me want to punch the fucker.

"I can't wait to see you fall," I shot back, staring down the man. Despite my pain, I refused to fail. "I'll see you again soon," I added, turning and heading to the high school. I caught a glint of metal in the fleshy ground, catching sight of the dagger. I stepped forward to go for it when the demon hooked an arm over my left and spun me, causing me to become dizzy.

"Woah, hang on," he said. "There's one last thing before you run off."

"You sure talk a lot," I commented, annoyed.

The demon laughed, seeming almost amused. "You're so ignorant," he said, gripping my shirt and pulling me towards him. But that's okay; it makes this all the fun," he added before reaching out and grabbing my right arm, forcing it out of the sling.

I screamed in pain, pushing my left arm into his chest, but his grip was iron-tight, completely overpowering me.

"Stop squirming," the demon hissed. He pulled on my right arm, and the skin that made contact with him started to itch. Then, my right arm started to numb, I was unable to feel it when he suddenly released, and I stumbled back, the numbing sensation fading away into... Nothing? My shoulder didn't hurt anymore?

"There we go; you'll have a real fighting chance now."

"Why did you do that?" I asked, surprised.

"It's no fun if you get eaten up too quickly; I want to watch you struggle with all your strength."

I was thankful my arm was okay now, but at the same time, I was concerned; it sounded like this demon just wanted to play with me like some kind of toy, and I was afraid I was falling right into its trap.

"Chop chop detective boy, the longer you just stand here, the less of a chance you'll find anyone alive."

My eyes focused on the demon, disgusted by his smile. I went to speak but held my tongue when he stepped backward. Within a second, he sunk into the ground. I guess he was done, and that was fine by me.

I can focus and start heading to the high school; I turn and walk over to the dagger and pick it up, surprised he hadn't taken it. Or was he able to? There are so many unanswered questions.

I slipped the dagger into the slit on my belt and then started to walk, it'll take me some time to get to the high school from this point, but I'll get there regardless.

My stomach is queasy; I know the demon isn't going to play fair though I do have a feeling what he says about everyone being in the high school building is faithful; he may want to play games and fuck with me, but at the same time, keeping somewhat true to his deal like a carrot on a stick seems to satisfy the thing.

Fixing up my arm in the process just so I had a chance says everything, he plans to throw some dangerous things my way and wants to watch me struggle.

Fuck, how did my life become so upside down?

16

I finally made it to the high school, standing before it, out of breath. The blood and pieces of skin that stuck to my clothing and skin from the encounter with the demon had dried up, causing my skin to be dry and itchy, my feet numb from all the slippery walking I'd been doing.

My clothing is probably going to be ruined at this point; I'm pretty glad I left Gary's notebook back with the others; I wonder if my gun would even work anymore if it hadn't gotten ruined by the swamp water, not like it would do any good against a demon. This dagger is the only defense I have.

I looked around the building with the skin stretching across it. Trying to determine where the door was located wasn't easy, but luckily, the front door did have steps, which looked like a small bump under the skin where I would presume the door would be.

I am really hoping to find Kane. I know it's biased and that the others need help, too, but I can't help but worry for him. Sydney's baby, of course, will be a priority, but Kane is who I want to find most of all.

Gulping, I step forward to the flesh-covered steps, pausing momentarily before placing a foot on the first step. Feeling the slippery surface, I hesitate but keep forward, slowly but steadily making my way to where the door is supposed to be.

My legs shook, trying to keep me in place, so I hurriedly pulled out the dagger and used it to slice away the flesh in front of the door. All I needed was one side, so I cut off chunks until I could see the red-stained door, using this chance to slice around and give myself plenty of space.

I wipe my forehead, already feeling exhausted. Even though my right arm was healed, it still felt weirdly numb, causing some trouble with coordination. I made due with it and still managed to make it work.

Pulling the doors open, a sauna-like warmth radiated from within. The air was thicker and smelt of spoiled meat, causing me to turn my head and breathe in the air outside. This is going to be difficult, but considering all I have gone through, I'm not going to back down now, so before I could change my mind, I stepped inside the school.

The light through the doorway I created helped me see a little flesh still covered over everything, which, at this point, was starting to look normal.

Stepping further in, I could see a hallway ahead of me, but I could only see so far into it. Without windows or any form of light, I'd be wandering around blind, so I dug into my jacket.

Didn't I have a light or something in my jacket?

I found my water-logged notebook and then my phone, which, after some fiddling with it, did not seem like it'll ever work again, damn. I put my phone away and checked the little pocket on the chest, finding my old yellow zippo from back when I used to smoke.

Biting my lip, I flicked it open, and after a few strikes, the flame ignited; luckily, the swamp water didn't fuck it up, thank goodness to my awful habit.

Now that I had this, it wouldn't be the absolute best. Still, I'd at least be able to navigate, so I started forward, Zippo in my right hand and dagger in my left, leaving the comfort of the light outside for the darkness.

The flame illuminated my shadow across the flesh-covered walls, creating a disorienting environment.

After walking for ten minutes, or at least what I presume to be ten minutes, time felt different inside this place. Despite that, my legs were growing tired, and I'd been walking in a straight line this whole time; there must have been a turn at one point.

I turned around, and there was nothing but a stretch of hallway. I went to school in this building, so I knew there was a right turn at one point, but not this far down. This school wasn't even that big; is it somehow being manipulated? I mean, this demon did cover the whole town in skin and dragged Kane into the ground, so I suppose this wouldn't be that far off.

But that also means I need to consider my moves. There are classrooms, and I have yet to see a single door, which means, much like the front door, it's hidden. I should have known the demon would stoop this low.

It will take ages to find a single door, much less anyone.

Taking a few deep breaths, I remind myself to stay focused. Holding my zippo, I bring it up against the right wall, watching the skin twitch beneath the flame's heat. "Creepy," I thought.

Walking further down the hall, I tried to listen for any form of noise. If anyone was in here, maybe I would hear them? That is, if they weren't out cold. But this was the best idea I had when suddenly, I heard a whimper behind the wall.

"Hello?" I asked, bringing the dagger to the wall and testing for any soft spots

"Hello?!" it sounded like Declan.

"It's Mill," I told him, finding the doorway. The blade slipped into the flesh, and I cut around a large circle, the flesh falling with a squelch. I brought the zippo to the hole to see a dark room; Declan stood inside, Simon on the floor by him.

"Oh, thank god," Declan spoke, rushing over to me, almost falling as he slipped a little

"Hang tight," I told him, cutting away more to make an entrance. "Is Simon okay?" I asked, stepping into the room.

"Sort of. We've been here for so long and haven't eaten. He's taking it harder than me."

I knelt beside Simon, who opened his eyes to look up at me, the zippo helping illuminate the small room.

"It'll be okay," I reassure him.

"I knew you'd come for us," Simon coughed out. Despite his weakened state, he smiled, a little hope shining in his tired eyes.

"Let's get you two out of here," I spoke, slipping the dagger back by my belt, the zippo still in my left hand.

"Help me out," I tell Declan, taking Simon's left shoulder.

Declan rushed over and helped take his right, and we both helped him onto his feet.

"The front door isn't too far; I'll get you two as far as the exit then,"

I was cut off when all of a sudden the ground below us started to sink.

"Fuck" I shout, pulling Simon back, but Declan stays where he is, his feet stuck in the ground as he sinks in further.

Simon fell on top of me, my zippo tight in my grip, so I luckily didn't lose it, but it did go out due to the sudden gust from me falling.

Declan screams in the darkness, causing my heart to pound in my ears as I panicked, trying to light my zippo again with the weight of Simon on me, my left arm hooked around him to ensure he stayed in place. He wasn't doing so well, and I wanted to keep him off the ground.

After multiple strikes, the zippo finally comes back to life, illuminating the room; I quickly look for Declan with no luck; a large hole in the flesh had appeared where he once was, though.

How am I supposed to save everyone if they get snatched from me the second I find them? Looking down at Simon, he was awake but not responsive. I have to get him out of here. I can come back for Declan once Simon's outside.

Hurriedly, I shifted, taking Simon's right arm and pulling it over my shoulders so I could semi-carry him out. He was a lot taller than me, and unfortunately, I didn't have enough energy to lift him fully.

"You'll be okay," I told Simon, carrying him to the door, his feet dragging behind me. My body was shaking from under the weight while I held my right hand out with the only source of light we had when I felt the floor below me squirm and move.

Looking down, the flesh bubbled and rippled before moving and sliding toward the hole in the room; I gasped and fell to my knees, unable to stay balanced.

Simon fell beside me while the flesh carried us further into the room; I grabbed Simon's arm and tried to dig my heels downward to no avail.

I looked around the room, trying to find some way to escape this fate, but there was nothing; I couldn't do anything, so I did all I could do. I tightened my grip on Simon's arm and shut the zippo white knuckling it as I brought it to my chest just before we fell.

Disoriented, we free-fell down the hole, my arms brushing against the slick flesh of the walls, my grip on Simon's arm tight as I fell head first. Given the speed of our fall and how long it took us to hit any bottom, I didn't think we would survive this fall, at least until I felt the hole turn. It went sideways, and suddenly, it became a slide, a disturbing one, but one nonetheless.

Eventually we stopped sliding and I lay on my back, still holding onto Simon's arm and the zippo. Feeling like things had calmed down, I lifted my right hand and flicked the zippo on.

The room we ended up in was the same as before; the hole in the wall from which we had come in was still present. I turned my head around to see there was no door; looks like I'd have to find the way out again.

"How are you holding up, Simon?" I asked, illuminating where he was. I swear my heart stopped when I saw I was holding only his arm, the rest of Simon gone.

I flung the arm in a panic; the sound it made when it fell caused me to gag, clenching my chest to try and settle my heart.

"Fuck, Simon!" I screamed, turning to the wall and where the hole was. I had held onto him the whole time; where the fuck... How the fuck?!

"I. . . I need to find him," I spoke, but I didn't move, paralyzed.

This was becoming hopeless. Can I really do this? I was out of my element. It was foolish to think any of us could handle this.

I'm just a human; I'm nothing compared to this demon. Even with the gift from Dux, I was useless.

I laid back against the flesh, my zippo still on as I lazily held it in my right hand.

I just. I needed to close my eyes for a second.

17

I don't know how long I had slept, but when I opened my eyes, there was nothing but darkness, my zippo no longer in my hands. God, it was warm; my clothing stuck to me due to the sweat, my breathing raspy, and the air smelt of smoke.

When I tried to move, my limbs didn't work, though I didn't really care. A cloudy feeling washed through my mind, so any of these issues were so small to me; Why was I here? I didn't want to leave, it was so comfortable.

"Mill!" someone called out from so far away, were they calling out to me? Mill... That sounded so familiar.

I stayed still, not willing to move; Why would I? The name was called out again, this time closer. Whoever it was is making a racket when suddenly I felt a pressure release from my chest.

"Hang in there," the voice spoke from above me. I felt more pressure release from my body until I could see again.

Heat radiated in the room while Kane knelt over me, chunks of flesh in his hands; disoriented, I looked down at myself, realizing the flesh that covered everything had grown over me, trapping me against the floor, my mind becoming clear again as he set me free.

"Are you okay?" Kane asked, helping me sit up; he was shirtless, his hair a mess, and his shoes gone.

"I... I think so?" I groggily spoke, my voice dry

"That'll have to do," he said, helping me to my feet.

I stood shakily, looking at him then around the room, realizing that the veins in the flesh around us glowed a dark red, allowing us to see; why didn't they do that from the start?

"What happened?" I asked

"I woke up here and have been wondering for a long time until I found you."

"How did you know it was me?" I asked, looking down at where I had laid, a shiver running up my spine; I can't believe I almost gave up like that

"It was a hunch, I'm glad I was right."

"I am too," I said, grateful that it was he who had found me. "Have you seen Declan or Simon?" I asked, the image of Simon's arm still present in my mind. Where had I flung it? I felt terrible about that, but the panic I had felt in that moment was immeasurable.

"You're the only person I've seen."

"I think we're being scammed. The demon forced me to make a deal and I'm positive he's keeping everyone away from us so we can't win."

"What do we do then?" Kane asked

"We go after the demon himself," I replied, pulling the dagger from my belt. "This won't stop until he's dead."

"I'll help in any way I can," he said, placing a hand on my shoulder. I could tell he eyeballed my suddenly healed shoulder but said nothing, turning from me to the doorway. "Let's get out of this room."

I nodded, glancing down at the floor. The red light was still dark, but we could at least see. My Zippo is gone, nowhere to be seen.

"Let's go," I say, walking to the door. "How did you make this doorway anyway?" I asked

"It was already here; I thought you made it."

"I didn't," I replied, turning to look in the room one last time. The hole I had come in from close up.

"Well, I'm glad it opened up. I feel a hell of a lot better being at your side again."

"I am too," I admitted, my anxiety a little better knowing he was alive.

The hallway we walked down was illuminated in dark red, the veins along the skin pulsating like a heartbeat.

"How do you propose we find the demon?" Kane asked me

"We could insult him," I suggested, stopping in my tracks. I turned around and took in my surroundings. I was becoming tired of the skin and missed the feeling of being clean.

"Do you think insulting him would make him show up?"

"I'm not sure. I'm honestly just pissed off," I replied, taking in a breath of air and shouting, "Hey, you piece of shit! Show yourself, you coward!" it felt pretty good getting my frustration out.

"I don't think he's going to just show up if we start calling him names," Kane spoke.

"Who knows, his ego might be large enough," I replied, pinching the bridge of my nose.

"Come on, let's keep walking. There has to be something around here."

"Yeah, we can do that," I tell him, proceeding down the hallway again.

The red hue strained my eyes, causing me to close them longer when I blinked in an attempt to prevent the growing headache.

"Dead end," Kane suddenly said, stopping. I looked ahead to see the wall of flesh blocking our path.

"That's inconvenient," I mumbled, stepping forward. I slipped the dagger into the wall, hitting something hard. "I can't cut through; we need to turn around," I told Kane, turning only to see another wall down the hall.

"Wait..." I started

"Maybe it's just an illusion," Kane tried to convince himself, running down the hall, getting about halfway before slipping and falling.

"Careful!" I shout, following after him and kneeling to help him up.

"Thanks," He said.

"Just be careful," I replied, walking further down the hall to the blocked path we had come from. I don't blame Kane for panicking; I was a little Claustrophobic, too. Taking the dagger, I tested the wall to no avail.

"I can't cut through this one either."

"Mill!" Kane gasped out, slapping my shoulder

"Ouch, stop that," I told him, turning around to see the other wall had moved closer. "Is he trying to crush us to death?"

Kane breathed heavily. "Oh god, we're goners!" he panicked

"Woah, settle, we're not dead yet." I shook his shoulders, turning to the wall again. It had moved again, our space quickly becoming smaller.

Nothing was around us; the walls were too rough for me to cut through, but maybe... I looked down at the floor. "Watch the walls," I told Kane, dropping to my knees, praying this would work.

"What are you doing?" Kane asked, but I ignored him; the dagger sliced into the floor with ease, so I started to cut a circle, blood pooling around me, causing an itchy sensation to form, but I kept going.

"It's getting closer, Mill; please hurry!" Kane begged, kneeling down across from me.

I tried not to overthink how I was doing this or the impending doom coming for me. As I focused on making an exit, the flesh I cut out fell down into the ground, so I looked down into the room, the red hue showing what I presume to have been a classroom; the drop looked painful but not deadly.

Looking up at Kane, his wide eyes staring off, I looked both ways. The walls were closing in, so I gripped Kane by the arm and pulled him into the hole. He screamed, then yelped; I followed suit.

I fell right on my back, the pain causing my vision to blur, almost blacking out. Blinking and breathing heavily, I managed to keep myself conscious, Kane on his side beside me before he rolled onto his stomach, the skin beneath us nothing but a nuisance at this point.

I watched the hole above me as the walls collided; it would have crushed us if we didn't get out, but at what cost? I think my back was permanently broken, fuck.

"You alive?" Kane asked

"Sadly," I replied, regretting many of my choices up to this point, one of them not having a cup of coffee at Wallec's bar. Why was I thinking about this now? I shouldn't have any regrets. I'm still alive, and I will stay alive; I just need to move, the pain in my lower back flaring, though.

In the darkness behind me, I suddenly hear someone clapping slowly

"You two are pretty clever; I honestly thought you would be dead by this point," an all too familiar voice echoed in the room.

I groaned, forcing myself onto my stomach to see that goddamned demon, a cocky smile across his lips.

"You piece of shit," I hissed, just in case he hadn't heard me from earlier.

"Don't be like that, Mill; I thought we were having fun," he spoke

"I don't think you know what fun means," Kane mocked, standing up.

The demon laughed, watching us with a hungry gaze. "You were looking for me, weren't you? Well, here I am."

He was mocking us—I knew he was. His little trap failed, so I bet this was his way of finishing us off. Well, I won't let that happen. Breathing heavily, I forced myself up with shaking arms to stand beside Kane.

"I admire you, I really do, but you already lost your spot in my team," the demon told me, turning to Kane. "How about you, pipsqueak? Turn on your boss, and you'll receive everything you've ever desired."

I glared and went to speak but held back when Kane scoffed

"I got what I want; I'll never side with a monster like you."

The demon became furious, gritting his teeth as he narrowed his eyes. "You two are fucking pathetic! I can give you anything you could ever desire and you turn it down like idiots!"

"You're the dumbass for thinking we'll fall for your traps," I remarked, which only seemed to piss him off more.

"I'm going to enjoy killing you both," the demon growled

I lift the dagger up. "I dare you to try," I taunted.

The demon grew a wicked grin before shifting his feet slightly.

"Mill!" Kane shouted, pushing me; I fell onto my poor back, gasping from the pain, but kept the dagger tight in my left hand, looking towards where Kane's skin had grown, trapping his right leg.

"T'sk, so annoying," the demon spoke, walking towards Kane.

"Once you're gone, killing your boss will be easier."

I struggled to get back on my feet. My back was killing me, but I wasn't going to give up, not now; on shaking legs, I readied the dagger and charged while he was preoccupied with Kane, though I slipped on the skin at the last minute and ran right into the demon knocking us both down.

I landed on top of him, so I used this chance to run the blade into his chest, he screamed using his right hand to vice-grip my left arm and force it backward, I used my right hand to grip his throat, trying to choke him, but all he did was smile.

"I don't need to breathe," he mocked, punching me in the face and knocking me off, quickly sitting on me to keep me on the floor; his right hand kept my left pinned with the dagger while his left went to my throat, squeezing.

"I know you mortals do, though." he laughed. "When are you ever going to learn you can't beat me?" he spoke, slamming my left arm down against the floor until I was forced to drop the dagger, his grip on my throat tight, making it impossible for me to speak.

"Maybe I should take my gift back," he spoke, looking down at me with a shit-eating grin; I opened my mouth, but I only wheezed, his grip tightening as spots formed.

"You don't get to talk anymore," he growled. His grip on my left arm loosened as he swapped hands on my throat to take my right arm, confused before a burning sensation started.

Realization hit me by what this gift was, as a shooting pain shot through my shoulder as if I was shot all over again, I tried to yell out in pain, but I couldn't make a sound the demon laughing.

"Isn't this fun?"

I gagged, pushing against his chest with my left arm, trying to get him off of me to no avail. He was so strong, my vision blurred.

"You're going to feel this pain for all eternity; I'm going to make sure of it," he said, laughing, enjoying every little bit of this.

I claw at his face, trying to fight back, his skin ripping off and falling on me, exposing his tendrils and veins, his right eye falling out.

"Maybe I'll skin you alive and take your skin like a suit," he threatened

Oh god, is this it? His grip is just about crushing my throat; I can feel myself slipping; I can't believe I failed everyone. I went through so much, but for what? To be choked to death; what is he going to do to Kane?

At least Marshmellow will be okay; I'm so thankful I left her behind, so she didn't have to witness my death.

My vision completely went dark, my struggles growing weak as I felt myself slip, the echoes of voices invading my mind and calling me home.

I felt myself floating in a void, the pain racking my body from before when all at once, I suddenly took a breath, waking up on the cold, fleshy floor, my head pounding as drops of blood fell on my face.

Looking up at the demon, I saw the end of a dagger poking out of his chest, shock present on his face as Kane kicked him down, got on top of him, and started to stab him repeatedly.

Blood squirted everywhere as the demon's flesh melted away, letting out a high-pitched scream, struggling, but Kane was relentless; blood splattered on his face and body; he didn't stop until the demon's chest was nothing more than a puddle of blood.

I gasped out, breathing heavily, having just watched this take place, realizing Kane's right leg was skinned, blood trickling down it; he had forced himself free at the cost of skinning himself in the process.

I slowly sat up despite my body's protest to watch Kane take the dagger and stab it down the demon's face multiple times, making him unrecognizable before he finally stood up, the demon's body melting into a puddle of blood; Kane wiped his face smearing the blood before turning to me with wide eyes.

18

It's been a rough year since the incident with the demon; after Kane turned him into a bloody puddle, we had succeeded, at least, in killing him.

We still lost a lot of people that day; Sydnye's child was never recovered. We searched for days, but by day ten, we were pretty confident he didn't survive; she left town soon after that.

Due to my shoulder injury, I had to stay some days in a hospital, but I had Kane to keep me updated. I'm back home now, which is nice.

"Mill!" Marshmellow's voice pulled me from my writing, the words on my leather-bound journal blurring as I turned my head to the left to look at her. "Hmm?" I answered

"You have that meeting with the chief, remember?"

"oh shit," I said, turning back to my journal; I had forgotten about the meeting ever since the incident. Kane and I had been put on supernatural duty.

With the veil wide open, we get a lot of guests in our little town, and it's up to us to keep the balance.

"is Kane even here yet?" I asked her

"He says you better come eat the pancakes he made, or you're getting them cold."

"he cooked a whole meal, and you're just now getting me?"

"he did call for you, but you were so focused on your book."

"Simon told me it'll do me good to start writing," I explained, even though it felt pretty silly.

"Well, come get some food before you're late."

"I'll be right out."

She purred at my response and bounded out of the room.

I smiled softly, shutting my journal. Glancing at my wooden desk, the stack of books on supernatural creatures pilling pretty high, my blue mug void of any coffee, I sat facing the wall beside the door, a picture of Marshmellow above me.

My bed, still pushed against the window, had all-new red bedding with new pillows. My dresser was also replaced, and the closet was cleared out so that only my things were there.

It wasn't easy, but Kane had helped clear out a lot of things. I sort of had to do it when the demon was killed. The skin didn't exactly go away on its own... We had a lot of cleanup. The wild helped in a way. You'll find bird nests with the skin stuck in twigs and bushes; the larger predatory animals would even eat some.

Needless to say it's been a weird time for everyone. We had a lot of funerals during the first few months. They all felt so empty with everything going on. It was a struggle to be there emotionally; Poppy's funeral has been the hardest.

Sighing, I pushed myself up from the desk and walked to my dresser, changing into blue jeans and a white tank top with a yellow button-up.

Taking a look at myself in the small mirror beside the closet, I brush a finger along my cheek. My clean shave still looks nice, and my curly hair is extra fluffy—that stuff Kane gave me does wonders.

When I left my room, the smell of freshly cooked pancakes filled the hallway. Ever since he's been coming over more often, my fridge has been stocked and he cooks pretty frequently.

Taking a quick glance into my living room I saw the new TV sitting on its old stand with a new plush couch in front of it. The coffee table had been replaced with a larger one. The sliding door shut tight with duct tape. The fairies had taken a liking to my yard, and I can't lose another muller.

Shuddering at the memory, I turn to the kitchen, the family pictures hung up along the walls. Inside the kitchen, I haven't done much with it quite yet, so it still stands the same.

A plate of pancakes and bacon sat on my table with an array of syrups and some butter.

"You outdid yourself," I tell Kane, seeing him standing in front of the fridge and shutting it.

His dark brown hair has grown to his shoulders; currently, he has it back into a bun. His milky brown eyes are full of light, as always. He wore tan cargo pants with a button-up blue shirt.

"You're going to see the chief in that outfit?" I questioned

"It's not like I need to impress her," Kane said, smiling at me. "Plus, it's damn hot out."

"It has been warm lately," I agreed, looking out the kitchen window. Most of my lawn is cleaned up, but I can still see chunks of rotting flesh stuck to trees.

"Eat up," Kane said, sitting at the table and grabbing some pancakes.

"Shouldn't we be heading out?" I asked, sitting down and taking a piece of bacon

"We have a few minutes now, stop worrying," he said, standing up and grabbing the entire coffee pot and pouring me a cup.

"Oh, thank you," I say, smiling, taking it, and proceeding to burn my tongue trying to take a sip.

"Careful," Kane said, placing the coffee pot back and returning to his seat. Marshmellow was probably off in her room. I had changed the loft into her personal space with a TV and the works. She really likes watching science shows.

"What do you think the chief wants?" I asked Kane, grabbing a pancake for myself.

"I bet it's the gnomes; they've been causing quite the trouble."

"You provide them with a little sugar, and now you can't keep them out of the shops."

"at least some of them took up jobs."

"They definitely helped fill in the gaps. . ." Kane said. Silence fell over us as we each ate some of our food, knowing why there were so many gaps. Nora and Debbie were the two main people who worked at the shop. Nora died, and Debbie was never found. Then, we were left without a makeshift when John died.

The Boss was never found when everything cleared up, and neither was Luke or Mike.

Without a trace, we can't even find them; the gnomes offered to help but nothing came out of it, they just simply vanished.

"We should get going." Kane broke the silence when he had finished his pancake

"Yeah, you're probably right," I replied, standing up. I took my cup and drank the last of my coffee.

Wiping my mouth, I placed the cup in the sink and walked out to the hall. "We'll be back soon!" I called out to Marshmellow

"Bring home milk!" she called back from the living room, so I turned to Kane.

"Don't we have milk?"

"There's only a little bit left," he replied, so I turned back to face the living room.

"Okay, we will; see you soon," I said, turning to the front door.

I slip on my somewhat worn red sneakers. My still-new light blue overcoat fits me a little snugly compared to my old one, while my new brown Fedora has a blue feather to the side of it and a pretty blue patch along the rim.

My old clothing had gotten pretty ruined, so I updated my wardrobe.

"Weren't we talking about how hot it was outside?" Kane asked, tugging on my overcoat as he walked past me to open the door, a cool breeze hitting me.

"It's my signature look."

"It'll be your signature death outfit when you have a heat stroke," he teased.

"You're just jealous," I teased back, following him outside.

The sun bore down on me, but I didn't say anything out of spite so Kane wouldn't call me out.

Our new cars are parked out front. We had to get new ones because the skin had destroyed about every vehicle in Northwood.

I had gotten a simple silver Chevy, while Kane chose a larger blue truck.

"Let's take mine," I tell Kane, walking to my driver's side

"Alright," Kane replied, striding over to the passenger seat.

Twisting my keys that were already in the ignition, my car started with a stutter.

The Northwood radio station came on with the radio, Alex's voice coming through.

"I hope you all enjoyed that last song. I have a report from the station for an alert. If you are having bad dreams about the man with no face, call the police. If he occurs more than three times, it's too late, so don't hesitate to ask for help."

"Didn't you have that dream?" I asked Kane as I pulled the car back and headed to the main road.

"I did; Simon got rid of him, though, with his witchy stuff."

"Better than the goddamn fairies," I huffed

"I'm glad the fairies don't move close to town."

"Not like you stay at your own place anyways," I joked

"It's more convenient being at your place," he laughed.

I rolled my eyes but smiled still. A calm instrumental song came over the radio as the Jhonson's restaurant came into view as we passed it.

With the door locked and the windows boarded up, the building became a nesting ground for little spirits. Since Mike was never found, Bob didn't have the heart to keep it open.

So he closed it up and works at the local cafe. I don't think he's truly happy, but I see him there often, and I try to be there for him as best I can.

Having lost family also, I know what he's going through. I just wish I could do more to help him; focusing, I saw a shadow move along the trees; the damn Hide-Behind better not move too close to town.

Driving for another minute, I see the station, so I turn left into the lot, parking by the door as always; a few silver cars are parked.

I rub my eyes before getting out of the car, preparing myself to know what the chief wanted, Kane following suit.

Walking into the station lobby, nothing had changed besides who worked there. Declan has taken Poppy's job, so her office—his office—is arranged differently. With Benny missing, there is only one officer in the town, with Kane and me being detectives—honorary officers when needed.

Scarlet does help, but as the new head chief, she's been busy, especially with the whole supernatural situation we've had going on.

Walking to the office that used to be the Boss's that Scarlet took over, we walked right in the door wide open.

The inside was pretty empty. Scarlet had cleared away most of the pictures and things the Boss had. A large map of Northwood spread across the left wall, with little pins indicating different supernatural creatures and their homes for keeping track of.

The desk was cleared up, and a nice new monitor and PC were placed on it. A cute little cactus was on the corner of the desk, and the window was wide open, with a table in front of it lined with different potted plants. Scarlet had really made this space cozy.

She sat in a wheeled chair behind the desk, her long amber hair cut close to her skull. She wore a blue button-up shirt with dark blue jeans.

"Took you two long enough," she said, leaning back and crossing her arms.

"Sorry we got distracted," I told her, Scarlet looking over to Kane

"He forgot," Kane outed me, so I nudged his shoulder

"You're not in trouble," Scarlet chuckled, standing up. "The job I have for you two is pretty small, though I would appreciate you arriving on time," which, in code words, means I'm not in trouble now, but I will be if I'm late again.

"I won't be," I promised.

"Good," she said, walking to the map and placing a white pin on the grocery store. "The gnomes are saying something is stealing items from shelves; I need you two to head over and see what you can find."

"And if it's the gnomes stealing again?" I asked

"Well, they will be punished just like anyone else here; if they are going to live here in Northwood and among us, they must follow the rules."

"Okay, well, we will see what we can find," I tell her

"I trust you two will figure it out," Scarlet spoke, sitting back down at her desk. "Things have been insane, but I'm thankful I can rely on you two, Ryker and Declan have been pretty helpful, too,"

"I know Declan does good; it doesn't change that I still miss Poppy," Kane said

"We all do," I reply

Scarlet nodded, leaning forward to type on her keyboard. "we lost a lot of people; all we can do is pay respect and go on with our lives."

"I suppose," I said, knowing she was right. "We'll head out. Give me a call if anything comes up."

"Will do," she replied, not looking up from her monitor, so Kane and I left.

Making our way outside the station, I slightly paused outside the doors.

The hit Northwood took will forever change the way we live, some for the better and others for the worse. I will always be thankful for the help I received along the way. The dagger Dux had gifted me had its own holster on my right hip while my gun sat snug to my left.

"Mill, come on!" Kane called from my car.

"Coming!" I called back.